A Voyage Around My Pipe

A Voyage Around My Pipe

James Cowan

New Cultures Press
Minneapolis, Minnesota

"The world is not an amalgam of objects; it is a heterogeneous series of independent acts."
—Jorge Luis Borges

The paper used in this publication meets the minimum requirements of ANSI/NISO Z39.48-1992 (R 1997) (Permanence of Paper).

Text set in Minion Pro

The paper used in this publication meets the minimum requirements of ANSI/NISO Z39.48-1992 (R 1997) (Permanence of Paper).

Distribution Address:
New Cultures Press
P.O. Box 141035
Grand Rapids, Michigan 49514-1035

Visit us on the web at
www.newcultures.org

Printed and bound in the United States of America.

15 14 13 12 11   1 2 3 4 5 6 7 8 9 10

Library of Congress Cataloging-in-Publication Data

Cowan, James, 1942-
A voyage around my pipe / James Cowan.
     p. cm.
ISBN 978-1-59650-010-5 (alk. paper)
I. Title.
PR9619.3.C597V69 2011
823'.914--dc22

2010044702

New Cultures Press

Minneapolis, Minnesota

Contents

A Voyage Around My Pipe   9

The Man in the Astrakhan Hat   11

In the Heart of the Country   13

The Book of Knowledge   15

The Keepers of Sails   19

The Ice Palace   23

Garden of Delights   27

A Queen's Invocation   31

A Game of Draughts   35

A Face in the Stone   41

Interlude in a Temple   45

The Elixir of Life   49

A Singular Man   55

An Urban Ascetic   59

Where Less is More   63

The Bust of Nefertiti   67

The Wedding Ring   71

A Talking Forest   77

Journey to the East   83

Abelard's Epistle   89

The Skin of the Tiger   97

The Butterfly Man   103

All at Sea   109

A Voyage Around My Pipe

"You feel yourself evaporating, and you attribute to your pipe the strange activity of smoking you."
—Charles Baudelaire

*I*ts stem is sweet to the taste, and avuncular. Entering its narrow tunnel, I feel my body beginning to attenuate as I descend into the bowl. Already I sense that the darkness around me is but a foretaste of some mesmeric dream of which forgetfulness is no more than an unremarkable outcome. The truth is that this tunnel makes me feel elongated, a slender adjunct to life. Is it any wonder that I am no longer in the same body? My pipe, after all, is drawing me away from what was once a narcissistic belief in embodiment.

Ah, how tight it feels! Already I hear my voice echo back at me from some distant cavern. Like a pilot on the bridge I furiously spin the wheel, conscious that in doing so I am sending the craft that is me on a wide and circuitous voyage. Upside down, inside out—each sensation afflicts me with immediacy more in keeping with a cold shower than a voyage to the bottom of my pipe. The bowl beckons; I can hear its sooty song. The voice of countless plugs of tobacco burning in the pit of hell reaches me. It is anguish I hear, the anguish of souls stranded in an addictive storm designed to pulverize all sensibility. Tobacco becomes a gull's wings as it plunges towards the sea.

At last I spew forth into the bowl. I tumble, head over heels, into this cavernous tomb of charcoal. I clutch at stalactites of ash, each one blistering with the elusive heat of satisfaction. I burn, yes! I burn. My body is now a victim of the mysterious narcosis of belief. I see in each pulsating ember all the symptoms of an imminent volcanic eruption. Like lava and hot pumice I am about to be expelled from my bowl. But I do not wish to be:

9

something draws me back into this maelstrom from which gases and toxic odors emanate with all the abandon of houris.

So this is what it is like to be inhaled, I tell myself. What is now the essence of me is suddenly at the mercy of someone's need to breathe. I find myself mingling with oxygen as I struggle to retain some sense of my palpability as fire. My pipe, it seems, stands between consummation and me! It is the altar on which I sacrifice the listless tinder that has become the hallmark of my condition. No longer am I simply pleasure—or *intoxication*. I have become a burning incendiary of polygenesis, a sparkle of innumerable worlds infinitely arranged.

Let me recline in this exquisite grate where fire is inextinguishable, where the specter of death no more hides behind smoke. He alone is my master. So we converse. Amid darkened halls we ponder the soot of cessation. I know he wishes to lay hold of me and compress me into a diamond. But, I resist. As his equal (momentarily) I hurl back at him the flint that he offered me as part of our agreement. No, I say. It is not time. Not yet. When the occasion arises I will light my own pipe and inhale myself into oblivion. Do not worry, gargoyle of the guttering lamp, I am yours.

Such will be the words on my epitaph:

The drug that is life is too easily consumed.

The Man in the Astrakhan Hat

When he moved between the tables, it was always with the finesse of a cat. One became conscious of him entering the café; his gloves elegantly arrayed in one hand, in the other his ivory cane reminiscent of a chasuble. His hat, of course, sat jauntily on his head—which was, one assumes, only partly endowed with hair. To see him like this was to recognize the perturbations of a sensibility long used to doing battle with ennui. Could it be that this man in the Astrakhan hat had entered the café in the hope of remaining unnoticed?

Invariably he carried on his person a book. As coffee was laid before him that morning the man produced a small, leather-bound volume of what appeared to be a selection of Ovid's elegies. I assumed without thinking that they must be those that had led to the poet's exile on the shores of the Black Sea when—and to his utter consternation—Emperor Augustus had finally read them. Ribaldry and sexual intrigue have a way of bringing a man undone. In Ovid's case, the dandy around town had received his comeuppance! Still, I found it hard to identify the man in the Astrakhan hat with the verses of a long-dead, licentious poet.

I began to dream. In reverie, poems are as solid as stones embedded in a path. They lead us deep into that quarry which is a mask. In it we hide, solitude our friend, a child's knuckle game our only pastime. Up into the air the bones fly, their curvature a pastiche of light. As he read each poem, the man in the Astrakhan hat fondled the top of his cane as though it were a skull. I imagined Hamlet in Yorrick's grave, gazing upon what were once his dead friend's features. They, too, were contorted in a way that suggested a loss of self.

The man in the Astrakhan hat remained imperturbable. Nothing flustered him, not the coming and going of customers or the skeins of smoke about him, nor the rustle of newspapers passing between anonymous hands. His world was that of a Vesuvian love. Daily catastrophes in far-off lands meant little to him. Instead, Ovid's poetry lay about his shoulders with all the nonchalance of a cape. He could feel the interpenetration of this lonely poet's being, far away in Tomus on the Sea of Euxine.

So there it was: exile. The man in the Astrakhan hat squeezed the top of his cane so that his knuckles whitened. Whether in a bustling café in the city or in his apartment, he probably knew that his condition was incurable. He had caught the virus in his youth when every action then seemed to him to be a piece of verse. Now, like Ovid, he stood on a cliff overlooking the sea, wondering whether there was any possibility of return. Below, the fitful waters of memory splashed against rocks. Spume rose and settled on his face like snow. Salt air and the smell of fish succumbed to the shortness of his breath.

Suddenly I realized that this man was me. Lassitude had caught up with me unawares, and only now was I able to summon the energy to gaze upon these remnants. Sensibility was not enough, I concluded, to act as repost to any variegation that might be buried in stone. More was required: a sword needed to be thrust deep into neck of that heaving bull of repose. The man in the Astrakhan hat must have known this as he turned the pages of his book, caressing each word with utmost felicity. He knew, as obviously I didn't, that whatever slumbers in memory lives its own inimitable life.

In the Heart of the Country

The explorer struggled through the undergrowth towards a distant outcrop of rock. He had been traveling all day on horseback from his camp by a dry watercourse. All he had to guide him was a rough map that had been given to him by a local tribesman. In hushed tones the old man had informed him that a treasure lay in a cave somewhere along this escarpment. It remained to be seen whether he, the explorer, was capable of discovering what the old man felt might be worthy of sharing with his newfound friend.

The country had not been easy to traverse. Anthills as high as houses stood guard over the region. Contorted acacia trees reminded him of Siamese twins that he had once seen in a circus. Heat-waves shimmered above the ground, and the sight of distant lakes assured him that he was riding towards a mirage. Could a man lose himself in this no-man's-land of space, he asked? Or was he merely riding into an adverse predicament, like so many others? He soon began to realize that to indulge in hallucinatory experience was not a condition of the mind so much as entry into an unknown place.

The sound of his horse's hooves rung like a metronome on the stones, and his shadow rippled over the earth. Once he disturbed a kangaroo asleep under a bush. The animal hopped away towards the distant outcrop, its tail perfectly balanced, as if suspended in mid-air. The explorer wondered whether he was journeying to the end of the world—or whether the world as he knew it had exhausted its own imperatives. Either way, he realized that his sense of self had grown ever more precarious, as if it too had chosen to quit its shade.

Approaching the outcrop at last, the explorer spotted the opening to a cave half way up the slope. It reminded him of a cry of anguish, so wide was its grimace. It occurred to him then that even remote landforms feel a sense of loss sometimes, knowing that what they stand for is rarely honored. If a treasure lies in there, he told himself, then for too long its worth had been presided over by tears. Meanwhile, the explorer produced a kerchief from his pocket and wiped the sweat from his brow. His horse broke into a trot.

Dismounting at last, the man climbed the slope to the cave. It was the moment he had been dreaming of: to enter this place in order to claim a treasure made his journey all seem worthwhile. The old tribesman had been adamant—that which lay here would eclipse all the wealth he had ever imagined. What the explorer discovered however, at least initially, were piles of bones, a few skulls, and a sense that he had stumbled upon a place of burial. If this were the treasure that the tribesman had referred to, then surely he had been duped.

All at once the cave wall revealed its secret. A panorama of spirit-figures, painted in ochre and pipe-clay, was arrayed before him. Each figure intimated silence, since none possessed a mouth. Was this the tribesman's so-called "treasure"? The explorer was nonplussed, as he had hoped to find gold. Instead, what lay before him was a fresco unalloyed by verbiage. Initially, at least, he found himself at a loss for words.

I speak for you all, he said to the spirit-beings. At last! He had spoken for the gods. Their treasure, it seemed, was to invoke his awe. Clearly the tribesman had led him to this place of silent converse. From now on he must learn to treasure conversation with bones, for they held the key to every discussion he might in future have with himself.

In the heart of the country, it seems, caves such as this one are of particular report.

The Book of Knowledge

*A*fter a long drive in a bus, I reached a pink city standing on a plain at the foot of a mountain range. In the late afternoon the sun bathed its ramparts in a glow that reminded me of flamingoes. I tried to imagine what it would be like reaching this place after a journey across the desert. Little would be said, I decided, though many *salaams* might be offered by way of thanks. Such is the nature of havens.

I had come here to seek out a tome reputedly in the possession of one of its inhabitants. A bookbinder in Cairo informed me that the celebrated *Book of Knowledge*, known by many names in the past *(Libris sapientiae, Le livre de connaissance, El libro de saber*, etc.), was now in the hands of a scholar in the old quarter of this city. How it had come into his possession, however, the binder from Cairo was not at liberty to answer. All he could advise me with certainty was that the *Book of Knowledge* always chose its intended recipient, rather than the reverse.

Among its many owners over the centuries were the celebrated Moorish philosopher, Ibn Rushd, Sharif al-Idrisi, a geographer at the court of King Roger of Sicily, and Gemistos Plethon, the Byzantine sage who had introduced early Greek thought to the Florentines. It was rumored also that the *Book of Knowledge* may have been one of the three lost books of Pythagoras which had come into the possession of Plato long after the death of the celebrated philosopher of Croton. Though its provenance was uncertain, it was clear that the book enjoyed a wide and fruitful readership. Men swore by it—or at least it helped them to substantiate insights otherwise left unresolved. I had reason to believe that the *Book of Knowledge* contained a letter from Jesus Christ to King Abgar of Edessa, politely declining his request for an audience. If this were true, then it would be the only proof we have that Christ could write, and that an earthly prince of that period had recognized him as his suzerain.

At the entrance to the old quarter I was met by a guide. The man agreed to take me into the medina to meet with the scholar, Sheikh Mokhtar al-Said. I was informed that he lived in the Street of Shadows *(Derb Abidallah),* some yards beyond where yarn was dyed and hung out to dry. In my mind I could already visualize a rainbow hanging there in mottled light. According to my guide, Sheikh al-Said owned a bookshop specializing in Korans.

Past stalls selling sheep's heads and monkey paws we walked, stepping ever deeper into the old quarter. I began to ask myself why a celebrated book would choose its present owner from such an unlikely group of people. I told myself that its pages must be less than discriminating, given the limited aspirations of this city's inhabitants. No one, I told myself, who enjoyed sheep's testicles as repast could possibly understand the *Book of Knowledge.*

Eventually we arrived outside a booth at the far end of the Street of Shadows. An elderly gentleman sat cross-legged at the entrance, a book in his lap. He was wearing a white *djellaba* and a tiny skull-cap which seemed to accentuate the pointedness of his beard. When he looked up and saw me standing before him, the Sheikh gave a stifled gasp. I was unsure as to whether this was provoked by my sudden appearance outside his shop, or whether he was half expecting me anyway. Whatever the reason, Sheikh al-Said bowed his head gravely when my name was announced.

"You have come here," he said, "to learn more about the *Book of Knowledge.*" I was taken aback by the fact that he had already divined the reason for me being there. "Many men," he added, "arrive here in the hope that I might pass it on to them. The truth is, Monsieur, the book is not for sale."

To which I replied, "Is it possible to at least peruse it?"

Sheikh al-Said pondered my request for a short moment. As he did so, he wrapped his djellaba tightly about his shoulders. Weighing up his thoughts had become an exercise in patience for me. I began to suspect that the book might not exist, or that it had already found a new owner.

In any event, I reasoned, a letter from Christ to a king would have been of little interest to a Moslem scholar.

"Come back tomorrow," Sheikh al-Said urged. "In the meantime, I will consult the *Book of Knowledge* in order to see whether it is appropriate for you to study it." With that, the old man dismissed me and returned to his studies.

Back in my room on the edge of the medina I lay on the bed listening to the sound of drums in the square, and a muezzin calling the faithful to prayer. It was a hot night, and I found it hard to sleep. Later, a vision of the *Book of Knowledge* floating among clouds caused me to wake up with a jolt. It was as if its contents had become air! Then I realized how insubstantial truth is when subjected to analysis. Sheikh al-Said probably saw me as somewhat of an interloper in the field of speculation; I was more interested in acquiring knowledge than in its immediate dispossession.

In the morning my guide dropped by to take me to Sheikh al-Said's shop. Once more we passed sheep's heads on our way into the medina. Under colored yarn we walked, sensing that we had passed through a prism. When we reached the Sheikh's booth, I found to my consternation that it had been boarded up.

"The good Sheikh has departed for the mountains," a passerby informed me, stroking his beard. "It seems he felt in need of a dose of more rarefied air."

Suddenly I began to experienced breathlessness. My entire body seemed to contract. Could it be that I was suffering from the loss of what I had always desired? The *Book of Knowledge*, as coveted as it was, had slipped through my fingers before the opportunity to look at it had even arisen. Mountains, ramparts, and pink cities fought for my attention: they were the manifestation of a typology more in keeping with certainty than this non-appearance of a book, whose origin was both obscure yet vaguely disconcerting.

Could it be, I asked myself, that the *Book of Knowledge* was a more sublime text than ever I had given it credit? That it had passed through so many hands on the way to the present day suggested to me that the book was on a journey also. But, what kind of journey? Or was it more like a chameleon content to disguise its effects? To imply that the book was like a lizard or a vagabond was to place it in the context of metamorphosis, I realized. Its message was capable of changing every perspective a man might possess in keeping with his chameleonesque or vagabond nature.

No wonder Sheikh al-Said had departed for the mountains! He could not face the prospect of telling me that I had embarked upon a wild goose chase the very moment I had chosen to look for him. Stupid man! Mine was a journey in search of wisdom when in reality such wisdom could never be realized.

The *Book of Knowledge* was a smokescreen designed to protect all those who considered time irrelevant to their purpose. These men, I now knew— philosophers and sages, all of them—had found a way to choreograph their departure from the world. They simply *passed on* their knowledge by way of an exemplified text that masqueraded as a book, and so distanced themselves from all communion with others. The truth was that what they had learned in the course of their lives amounted to little more than a hodge-podge of facts, which in turn they at least had the good grace to recognize as such. The *Book of Knowledge* was no more than a delightful artifice created to confuse those who thought it could be owned.

I returned to my room on the edge of the square inspired by new purpose. From hereon I must devise my own *Book of Knowledge*, complete with the equivalent of sheep's testicles, monkey paws, and flamingoes as part of its contents. No one could deny that such similar objects might not provoke the next generation of bibliophiles eager to discover why, in real life, truth forever slips through one's fingers. This, surely, was the secret of the *Book of Knowledge*. No wonder Christ felt inclined to contribute to it with a letter no one has yet seen, since he alone had dispensed with gravity in the course of his tumultuous life.

The Keepers of Sails

On a journey to the interior of the island, high in the mountains, an anthropologist stumbled upon a race of people who lived in houses built like ships. He was astounded to find himself gazing upon what appeared to be a flotilla of *proas,* each of them earthbound, yet all graced by a superstructure that reminded him of sails. He began to wonder how these people might have washed up in this spot, unless of course it was as a result of some inordinate flood. Noah, it seemed, was not the only man to have run aground on a mountain! A race of princes and slaves appeared to have found a haven here on this mysterious island.

He resolved to document all that he saw. The local headman offered him one of these proas to use as his research centre. Each day the anthropologist climbed down from his ship and wandered about the village, interviewing as best he could with sign-language the people that he met. On raised platforms under granaries he whiled away his days conversing with old men, these guardians of the lore, in an attempt to understand the complex nature of a people whom he now dubbed as the "Keepers of Sails" (*Ardu en Kalai*). It was his way of identifying with those he now regarded as mariners of the forest.

They told him of how their forebears had come to the island from a distant place. In memory of their origin they had decided to build houses that reminded them of their migration. In doing so, the old men advised, they kept alive a sense of sailing to an unknown destination. It was very important to know that they were always ready to embark at the behest of a fair wind should any untoward threat impose upon them this choice. In other words, transience was a fundamental law of these people he called the Keepers of Sails. They made it their business to be always alert to the need never to quit all memory of themselves.

The anthropologist dutifully noted down their remarks. His fieldbook steadily filled with information of a magical nature. The calls of omen birds, for example, each a prefigurement of some duty or obligation, were quickly captured by him on paper. The knowledge that all the animals of the forest spoke a language which was instantly communicable to these villagers struck him as being of substantial import to the business of deciphering how nature and men lived as one. The verbiage of trees was as rich in aphorisms as any philosophic doctrine expounded by Greek or Chinese sages.

In time, the anthropologist found himself being seduced by the strange, mystical doctrine expounded by the old men. As a consequence, whenever he stumbled upon a python or monkey in the forest, he no longer felt in any way disconcerted as he announced to one of these creatures: "Your coils are my embrace," or "May I join you in the treetops?" A lightness of being soon overcame him; his body had become absorbed into the ongoing fermentation of the forest undergrowth and the invincible activity of insects as they performed their myriad tasks. To this the old men nodded their approval: they were more than content to see him setting sail across the ocean of the world. This, after all, was essential to their doctrine.

One day the old men summoned the anthropologist to the granary under which they sat to impart a secret to him. It was to do with the Tau Tau, those effigies of the dead that populated a string of cliffs some distance from the village in large burial enclaves. These effigies, they said, were the incarnation of their ancestors. Dressed in all their finery, the Tau Tau lived among the cliffs and caves as embodiments of the first historic family. Thus, everyone since the arrival of their forebears on the island was accounted for. The Tau Tau gazed down at the living from their eerie as sentinels from the past. Their role, it seems, was to oversee the daily conduct of ritual in the ordering of all social activity among the people.

"They embody all excess of joy," one old man gesticulated.

"They unfreeze our hearts," another spoke in signs.

The anthropologist wrote down these remarks verbatim. He was at pains to emphasize the unusual intermingling of sentiment and doctrine. He soon realized that the villagers lived a life that held no converse with categories. These people readily averred that a snake, a monkey, or their Tau Tau ancestors were their superior in matters of the heart. Their excess of joy, which was in part a manifestation of their mystical relationship with nature, found its origins in the notion that they were forever at sea, forever on a voyage of discovery. For the anthropologist, such a notion flew in the face of his own more prosaic universe.

In the final days of his residency in the proa, the man took to gazing through a window at the flotilla beached in the clearing. People below wandered from one to another like schools of fish. He sensed too that his skin had begun to grow scaly and somewhat oily, as if his body were undergoing a fundamental change in its makeup. He breathed with difficulty, sensing the presence of gills emerging from the side of his head. Could it be, he asked himself, that I am encountering some sort of transformation, and that I am no longer what I seem? He brushed aside his fears as no more than a figment of an overheated imagination. He blamed the Tau Tau, the forest, even the old men who had inducted him into their circle.

At dawn one morning, the anthropologist awoke to the sound of surf on a beach. He quickly dressed, then began to climb the outside of his house. With each step, and clinging precariously to the thatch, he felt himself to be climbing ever higher into the rigging. Already he could see an ocean of green as he climbed above the tree-line. The turmoil of the waves was punctuated by the screech of monkeys and the slithering movement of pythons.

"Land ahoy!" he cried out.

From the cliffs beyond, where the Tau Tau sat in silent cogitation gazing into space, an echo responded: "Sailor, beware!"

At this point, the anthropologist realized that his fate was sealed. He had become victim to an inner mutiny. Deliberately, it seemed, the Keepers of Sails had cast him adrift. They knew that he had yet to experience the solitary life of a castaway. Only then could he become a true effigy of himself. For him to be transformed into a Tau Tau, he must drown in a sea of his own making—a sea filled with the flotsam and jetsam of his own life.

Later that morning, one of the villagers discovered the body of a white man lying on the ground at the foot of his house. It was obvious that he had thrown himself from the mast. With some distaste, the villager placed his hand over his nose in order to ward off the smell of dead fish.

The Ice Palace

High in the mountains lie a number of alpine lakes formed from moraine during the Ice Age. To the local shepherds these lakes are fathomless, and in some unaccountable way they are thought to be linked by underground streams to the sea. One of these lakes, known as Laguna de Vacares, possesses a special mystery of its own. For it is here that an unwitting traveler wandering the alpine stock-paths might find himself taken up in his sleep, or when he happens to go down to the shore to quench his thirst, by a woman of insatiable passion. Her sole desire, it seems, is to transport her victim to a palace built at the bottom of the lake.

Her name is Ojos del Mar, or Eye of the Sea. She was reputedly a concubine of the king who built the underwater palace, who then mysteriously passed away. Ojos del Mar's way of seducing shepherds is to adopt the guise of a white bird that tempts men to walk to the edge of these icy waters. As soon as they plunge their hand into the lake to quench their thirst, Ojos del Mar reverts back to her original form as a water nymph, wraps her arms around them, and draws them into her embrace. The chill of the water combined with the warmth of her kisses cocoons the benighted traveler in her voluptuous web. He becomes frozen and unable to move, as if he has been placed in a jar of formaldehyde.

Then she drags him down to her submarine kingdom, her icy palace, and places him in a hall known as the Corridor of the Knights. Though unable to move or utter a word, he nonetheless is aware that others like him stand propped up against the walls on either side of the hall. Each man is the victim of Ojos del Mar's charms, and suffers acutely for it. They form one long unutterable scream of anguish, their potency drained from them, their will petrified, since they have lost the gift of discernment. It seems that each traveler has been reduced to the cipher of another's obsession.

The beautiful Ojos del Mar has made them serve her passion, their now contorted limbs a replica of her desire to transgress.

To break free from this submarine palace is all but impossible. Only Ojos del Mar, it seems, holds the key. If a man is to do so, then he must first conjure before him an image so refined that not even she can see it. This image is like a sliver of glass slowly turning in the air, glacial in its movement and claim upon emptiness. He watches it like a hawk its prey. Somehow he knows that he must shatter the image, using all the force and intensity of his gaze. To do so is to weaken the power of Ojos del Mar, and so release the bonds that bind him to her. The Corridor of the Knights thus becomes a battleground between an invisible fragment of unusual clarity, and the memory of that seduction which first dragged him down into this kingdom of ice.

A man is only able to escape the underwater palace and the charms of Ojos del Mar by a supreme act of renunciation. He must revert back to that man in league with the pure air of the mountains into which he had first stumbled, alone and unbidden, a traveler wandering aimlessly on alpine paths. He must turn his gaze away from the white bird soaring above, that temptress of the depths masquerading as his guide, and look towards the emptiness and clarity of the morning. This indeterminacy, this uncertainty becomes at once as a lamp illuminating an icon. Wariness is not an option. For him to escape imprisonment he must channel everything into one last act of submission.

It is the only way to escape that underwater kingdom and the ice palace of a nymph. Ojos del Mar is powerless against men who choose to concentrate their energies on observing the invisible nature of melting ice. Its *there*-ness, so to speak, becomes an act of retention for them, an anchor. Ojos del Mar has no alternative but to acquiesce when confronted by such a primary encounter with a man's solitude, and with his fearless nature. Resisting her seductions, he is finally able to overcome her every embrace. The lake no longer claims him. The Corridor of the Knights becomes an empty place, windy in aspect, home to escutcheons that depict aimless suffering only.

Alone among men, the wanderer is able to surmount his tendency to relinquish his greatest strength in the arms of Ojos del Mar. At this point she becomes no more than a pallid bird, a figment caught up in a web of her own making, lost amid eddies and whorls of her insatiable passion.

Garden of Delights

"A dream is like an animal, but an unknown animal,
and you cannot see all its members."
—Elias Canetti

Not far from the city of Canasia, near a monastery, lay a park surrounded by a high wall unlike any other in the world. Its gatekeeper was a monk who possessed the only key to this park, and whenever travelers arrived to meet the Great Khan, he gladly showed them around. Friar Francus, traveling as a papal legate to the Great Khan's court, happened to visit this monastery and its adjacent park one day. He has left a unique record of what he saw inside.

According to the good friar, the gatekeeper arrived at his cell door one morning bearing a basket full of meat and bones. He invited Francus to accompany him to the park outside the monastery walls. Presumably the food in the basket was for the creatures that lived inside the park. Unlocking the gate, the gatekeeper gestured to Francus to pass through into the broad green field that lay beyond. The good friar soon found himself gazing upon a steep mountain at the center of this field, together with trees and patches of verdure growing on the surrounding plain.

The gatekeeper then struck a note on a tiny set of cymbals in order to summon the creatures down from the mountain. In time strange animals, many thousands of them, descended the slopes and made their way towards the two men. Francus began to recognize among the horde certain figures that looked like apes, but he couldn't be sure. Even the monkeys and cats seemed quite different from what he had become familiar with during the course of his travels. Suddenly he understood why, for many of these creatures possessed faces that reminded him of men. In a state of agitation, and not a little fearful, Francus asked the gatekeeper who these creatures might be.

"They are the souls of noble men," he responded. "We continue to feed them for the love of God."

On further inquiry, Francus was able to ascertain that these half-human creatures were the result of an act of transmigration. Just as men of noble temperament entered the bodies of animals of a certain grace and deportment, so do men of brutish minds find themselves imprisoned in the bodies of vile and brutish creatures. Disputing this explanation, the good friar remonstrated with the guest master that it was impossible for men, when they died, to take on the form of animals in the afterlife. It was a heresy, he argued, to think that in death one was destined to become a distortion of some quality already existing in this world. But the guest master was adamant: as far as he was concerned, men were obliged to take on fantastical shapes when they died in order to reflect their conduct in life.

"No act performed in this life," the guest master insisted, "is ever diminished through death. We carry the sum of our anguish and joy into the world of darkness."

While the guest master handed out pieces of meat and bones to the throng of strange and often frightening creatures that milled about them on the edge of the field, Francus pondered both their predicament and his own. Their contorted faces and relief at being fed mingled in his thoughts. He suddenly realized that he wasn't looking at cat, lion, leopard, ape or tortoise so much as at virtues masquerading as creatures. Their hunger, and the anguish on their faces, was less the result of any individual lack on their part, as it was a desire to reinvigorate their original forms in life. They wanted to reconstitute some measure of the nobility and grace they had known before these had become diluted during the course of their passage into the other world.

"Our responsibility," the gatekeeper added, "is to ensure these men fulfill their task of remonstrating with memory."

The good friar was nonplussed by this remark. He couldn't understand how a man, in death, might wish to recall his condition in life, even if he had wanted to. Memory, after all, was a state possessed only by the living. To feed such creatures scraps of meat and bones from this life was to reinforce an absurdity also: no man—no creature—could hope to be revived by consuming bodily parts from one world in that of another. The two worlds simply did not mix. One was physical, tactile and memorable; the other was immaterial, untouchable and forgettable, since it didn't really exist. How could a creature masquerading as a virtue begin to embrace the dubious nature of its failure in this world?

When the creatures milling about had eaten their fill, the gatekeeper rang his cymbals to announce the end of the meal. The animals dutifully walked back towards the mountain, licking their lips. Francus was left with the impression that they were more than satisfied with their repast that day. It was like an elixir, a draught of the real, which allowed them to assume some semblance of what they thought they might have been.

"You see, brother Francus," the gatekeeper observed. "I have given them a taste for the past. This they can now digest at their leisure. It will sustain them for as long as they choose not to remember. Hunger, you see, is a condition of memory. Forgetfulness is derived from being sated."

Francus quit the park in a quandary. He had come here, he thought, in possession of more than a valid argument against transmigration and its attempt to merge two distinct worlds. In spite of this, he had learnt something new. The gatekeeper had invited him to observe its fantastical creatures, knowing that it couldn't possibly have existed. Then again, if it didn't exist, Francus realized that he had come away from the place visibly affected by what he had only imagined. This, he now knew, was all part of his wildest dreams.

A Queen's Invocation

In 947 A.D., the elderly historian Abu al-Masudi, after a lifetime of travel, decided to retire to Old Cairo in order to live out his last days. In his youth he had visited the lands of Syria, Iran, Armenia and the shores of the Caspian Sea, the Indus Valley, Ceylon and Oman in Arabia, as well as the east coast of Africa as far south as Zanzibar. Now an old man, he had allowed books to become his world rather than the memory of lonely rooms in caravanserais. Al-Masudi had written many of them during the course of his travels, including his most important, *The History of Time (Akhbar az-zaman),* an encyclopedic world history and compendium of all knowledge. In it, he recounted a story that confirmed his boldest premise: that words were more powerful than the things they represent.

According to al-Masudi, after the Pharaoh and his army were drowned in the Red Sea while pursuing the fleeing Israelites, the wives and slaves of these unfortunate warriors left behind felt themselves vulnerable to attack from their old enemies in Syria, now that they had no army to protect them. To forestall such an event, they elected as their queen a woman wise in the ways of magic. Her name was Dalakulah. Her first decree was to build a wall around the land of Egypt on which was inscribed crocodiles and other wild animals in the form of hieroglyphs. These, presumably, were to frighten off marauding bands of nomads unfamiliar with the power of inscription. Queen Dalakulah fondly believed that the hieroglyph was Egypt's greatest defense against invasion.

As a magician she also collected all the secrets of nature, as well as all the attracting and repellent powers she believed were contained in minerals. Practicing her sorcery with the aid of stars, she bestowed upon the effigies of her enemies fashioned from clay numerous spells which enabled her to orchestrate their destruction. When the armies of Syria or

Arabia set out to invade Egypt, she commanded their effigies be buried so that those they represented might suffer the same fate. By her actions, Queen Dalakulah ensured that the invading armies simply disappeared into the ground! It appeared that her magical formulae were capable of making things lose their substance, and so neutralize any negative effect which they might possess.

Al-Masudi was fascinated by what he had learned. He attributed to Queen Dalakulah remarkable theurgic powers. She was not a woman so much as a white magician. How could anyone make language capable of transforming inert objects into such powerful talismans? His own language of Arabic, which he firmly believed to be a sacred gift from Allah to his people, he knew had never been put to such a test—at least, not to his knowledge. Queen Dalakulah had obviously found a way to make words into primary vehicles for transmission. With their aid, it seems that anyone could protect themselves from evil, however it manifested itself. Whether it was an invading army or a false accusation, language became one's only sure line of defense.

When al-Masudi wandered down to the Nile to take the airs of an evening, he often pondered how Queen Dalakulah had been able to make language so talismanic. What was her secret, he asked himself? He had spent his whole life on the road, traveling from one country to another, trying to discover the mystery of Time—yet on no occasion had he been fortunate enough to meet with a sage able to inform him of how words might be imbued with that special quality denied even to Time itself. Life on the road was a transition, after all; so surely there was a prospect of gaining insight into what was the magical property of words. Only then did he recall reading a few lines from the *Fatiha Sura* ('The Opening') in Damascus long ago that perhaps elucidated his dilemma—and, moreover, confirmed Queen Dalakulah's supreme artistry as a theurge. From memory, then, he began to write down the relevant lines on a tablet as soon as he had retired to his rooms on a back street in Old Cairo that evening:

In the name of God, the Compassionate, the Merciful, let it be known that the spiritual world opens up vast perspectives, full of brilliant new possibilities, only when the mind is made impervious to the surface of all things in nature. Such, we must accept, is no more than an effigy of the world. Thus we must be ever alert to the essential nature of how we perceive, and so not be seduced by that which is observed.

In doing so, the aridity of grammar is finally overturned and becomes an evocative sorcery. Words are able to rise from the grave clothed in flesh and bones, the substantive in its substantive majesty; the adjective as a transparent garment which clothes and colors it like a glaze; and the verb, that angel of movement, which sets the sentence in motion.

This, O Compassionate One, is the secret pertaining to the power of words. They are able to move mountains, and so destroy the vast armies of ignorance arraigned against us. Let it be known that language is a bastion upon which we view the world from a safe haven.

Satisfied that memory had not failed him, Abu al-Masudi put aside the tablet and his writing instrument. Outside, he could hear the muezzin calling men to prayer. The Sura's declaration mingled with that of the man uttering the *bismillah*, "In the name of God, most gracious, most merciful." All about him, it seemed, words were darting back and forth like houris. These angelic beings were more than effigies, he realized. They were none other than Dalakulah's attendants, the wafting and rhythmic embodiment of being as it shed all constraints.

Could it be, he asked himself, that the mysterious formulae used by the queen to protect her kingdom were in some way linked to words as the mystical embodiment of numbers? After all, he reasoned, certain letters in Arabic known as the "prefatory ones" or "detached letters" *(fawatih)* can be added or subtracted, each according to design. Perhaps the hieroglyphs of old were complex formulae which had the power to reduce all letters to zero, and thus eliminate at a stroke the vast armies of Syria and of Arabia outside the walls. It was a worthy thought.

All it required now was for him to believe in this premise. In his mind, the world of things became subservient to the way in which it was expressed. Words were seen to be more real in that they were the garment of the unseen. Al-Masudi tried to imagine them as a cloak, a pair of sandals, the many folds of his burnoose. He began to see himself walking the back streets of Old Cairo dressed in a *gallibiya,* shielded by a baldachin woven from damask and shot through with silk, while being borne aloft by slaves. He found himself surrounded by all the bliss of adjectives, the robust congruity of nouns, and the restless energy of verbs. They jostled like urchins pleading with him to toss them a few coins.

Suddenly he was no longer an aging scholar living in an alien city, but a man embellished by all the subtleties of language. He had become a sorcerer too, as well as the subject of his own sentence desperately seeking its object, a diacritical point in the huge expanse of the universe which might finally encompass the history of Time itself. No wonder he had been drawn to Queen Dalakulah as a model for his own endeavors. Her white magic, if that is what it could be called, was sufficient to bolster the defenses of the known with a most potent formula—that of the word being a mysterious entity capable of transforming every object it embraced into an untimely image.

Then it dawned upon Abu al-Masuda what the secret to Queen Dalakulah's sorcery might be. In the process of protecting her land she had discovered that each letter of the alphabet was the cohort of death. The word, as such, was the coffin in which the past was buried.

A Game of Draughts

"The bones and flesh which possess no writing are wretched."
—Unas Pyramid text

Numerous cosmologies have accounted for the origin of the universe, none better than that of the Hindu concept of an egg on the shoulders of an elephant standing on a tortoise. Our belief in the Big Bang theory and Black Holes, though more prosaic, gives us some hope that eventually we will find answers to this problematic question. The ancient Egyptians, with their penchant for death and the afterlife, devoted a good deal of thought to this same question, and devised some interesting theories of their own. One theory, which may be likened to that of a Russian doll, intimates that the universe is made up of a series of universes, each encased within the next. Thus, to give it a more modern interpretation, the stratosphere encloses the atmosphere which encloses the biosphere then the ecosphere—and so on, until the atom is glimpsed.

During the New Kingdom, a prince called Setnau Khaum-Uast spent much of his time studying the power of amulets and talismans in his library. His father, who was Pharaoh, allowed his son to pursue his studies, believing them to be efficacious to the overall health of the kingdom. Setnau amassed a library of papyri on these subjects, and was often consulted by wise men eager to learn more. Sometimes they would gather in his library, known as 'The Double House of Life,' in order to talk with this remarkable prince.

"Can a man possess magical powers simply by reading a book?" one asked.

"Is eternity a word or a place?" another inquired.

"There is a book," replied Setnau, attempting to answer both questions with the same response, "that contains certain charms able to entrance heaven, earth, as well as hell. To address your question, however, I will tell you how the recital of one charm in particular enables a dead man to rise from the tomb and resume his life on earth."

The sages smiled knowingly, believing that to resume life after death was an illusion. Nonetheless, out of courtesy, they asked the prince to inform them as to where this book might be.

"In the tomb of Ptah-nefer-ka, at Memphis," Setnau affirmed, and then went on to recount his story:

"In order to discover this book I went to Memphis to find the tomb of Ptah-nefer-ka with my brother, Anahaherurau. For three days and nights we dug in the necropolis nearby in the hope of finding his tomb. We eventually located it, and I was able to remove the stone blocking the entrance by reciting a secret formula. The earth suddenly opened up before us, revealing a tunnel into the tomb. We climbed down, inching our way to where Ptah-nefer-ka's coffin lay."

"And?" one of the sages urged Setnau to continue.

"As we entered, the tomb was illuminated by a mysterious green light. The walls filled with hieroglyphs seemed to glow. When I looked for the source of this light, I realized that it was coming from a book lying beside the coffin. To my consternation, I understood that we were not alone in the tomb. Ptah-nefer-ka's wife and son, at least their spirit doubles, sat beside his coffin. They had come to live with their husband and father as a result of a miracle enacted by Thoth, the god of words."

"Did you ask them for the book?" another sage asked.

"Ahura, Ptah-nefer-ka's wife, pleaded with me not to take away the book, informing me that to do so would prove my undoing. To reinforce her remarks, she told me the following story:

"'My husband,' she said, 'spent all his days in his library studying, once I had given birth to our son, Merhu. He wanted to know the secret of eternal life. A priest of Ptah promised to reveal to him where he might find the book you see here now, provided he give the man a hundred pieces of silver and two coffins. When these were handed over the priest duly informed my husband that he would find the book in an iron box at the bottom of the river at Coptus, on the Nile.'

"'The iron box is encased in a bronze box,' the priest explained. "The bronze box is further enclosed in a box made from palm-wood. Once you have opened this box you will find another made from ebony and ivory, which contains one made from silver. Finally, the silver box contains a box made from gold in which the book lies. But beware—the iron box is surrounded by swarms of snakes and scorpions bound together by a snake that cannot die.'

"'Not to be dissuaded,'" Ahura continued her own story, "my husband allowed myself and Merhu to accompany him on a royal barge to Coptus. There he went to the temple of Isis to offer libations to the goddess. As a reward, the high priest made him a model of a floating barge upon which numerous workmen were arranged. These came to life as soon as my husband pronounced a magical formula upon their heads. It was they, you see, who discovered the iron box after diving into the river for three days and three nights.'

"'My husband succeeded in dispersing the snakes and scorpions surrounding the iron box with a charm. The snake that cannot die he cut into pieces twice before it eventually died after a third attempt. Finally he open the iron box, then the palm-wood box, followed by the ebony and ivory box, the silver box and lastly the gold box. From that box he drew forth the book you see here now. It was a moment to be savored.'

"'Back on the royal barge my husband, Ptah-nefer-ka, lay down to read the book. He studied the magical formulae that so enchanted earth, heaven and hell. He did the same with a second magical charm so that he might see the sun rising in the sky in the company of the gods. I too read the book at the behest of my husband, and I became privy to its secrets.'

"'My husband wrote down the secret formulae on a piece of papyrus and then waved incense over it. Later, he dissolved the papyrus in water and drank it, knowing that in doing so he had acquired forever the knowledge which was in this magical book. Little did he know that his action had aroused the ire of Thoth, the divine god of words. To possess all knowledge, it seems, was in contravention of his edict.'

"'His decree was that both I and my son should never return to Coptus alive. In a freak accident as we returned to shore, both of us fell overboard and were drowned. Sadly Ptah-nefer-ka, my husband, did not survive the voyage back to Memphis, either. The book had become our nemesis: we were destroyed because we knew too much.'"

"At this point," Setnau resumed his own story, "hearing Ahura's explanation, and in spite of the risks, my curiosity got the better of me. I asked Ptah-nefer-ka, who by now was reclining in his coffin as he had done on the royal barge, to hand over the book. I wanted to know its secrets, even if I did not wish to consume them like he had."

"Did he give you the book?" a sage asked.

"He insisted I play a game of draughts with him, and that the winner take all," Setnau replied.

"Which you did, of course."

"It was not easy. Ptah-nefer-ka tried to rig the game in his favor by cheating. In the end, he admitted defeat and handed over the book to me. I asked my brother to climb to the surface and bring back my own charms and talismans which I knew would help me to make my escape from the tomb with the book. When he returned I uttered them, and immediately found myself flying up through the earth with the book in my hands towards the heavens, surrounded by a mysterious green light. It was an exhilarating feeling. I was in possession of all knowledge, in spite of Ahura's fears for my safety. No one, not even Thoth, had power over me now. I had become immortal."

"And you believed it?" one of his guests asked.

Setnau nodded. "How could I not? The book had given me power over everything. I was the master. The heavens were open to me, and the gods were my friends. I had not even to open the various boxes or kill serpents to attain this trophy. All those worlds within worlds were but tinder to my fire! You see, my dear friends, I had solved the cosmic riddle."

"Well?" another sage demanded, eager to know more.

But Setnau lowered his gaze. Memory of the green light emanating from the book filled his thoughts. A tear appeared on one cheek.

"I was wrong," he said at last. "For I too had contravened the edict of Thoth. When I returned to the palace with the book after my journey across the wide expanse of the heavens, my father the Pharaoh summoned me to give account of myself. After I told him of how I had acquired the book that held the secret to the cosmos, he shook his head. "My son," he said, "you have gone too far in your investigations. There are some questions that need no answer. It is not for mere mortals to presume to know the secrets of the cosmos. We are its servants, and must not be tempted into dabbling in things that do not concern us.""

"A pertinent thought," one sage remarked. "It is a presumption on our part to believe we should know everything. What did you do next, O prince?"

"I took the book back to Ptah-Nefer-ka's tomb," Setnau replied. "My father had made me realize the risks of tampering with the inner workings of the cosmos. It was right that the book, if unable now to be returned to its iron box surrounded by serpents and scorpions, should at least remain beside the mummy of its present custodian. Death has certain rights over the word, after all. For it is these, when they are uttered without caution, that reveal too much. Only death can hold them in check, and so preserve what is their inherent strength. The book, rightly contained within its various boxes, will always and forever glow, this we now know. Once it becomes common knowledge to people like Ptah-nefer-ka and me, then the risks are obvious. We deny it the mystery and prerogative of remaining unknown. The cosmos is not a thing but a perennial, self-fulfilling ideal. If we take away its right to remain unknown, then what is left, pray tell, for others to dream of?"

The sages looked at one another, perplexed. It was the first time they had been asked to consider such a proposition—that the unknown, the book that lay in the gold box, should in fact remain *unread*. It flew in the face of their idea of consummation, of knowing the essence of things, which in part they were dedicated to achieve. It suggested, too, that there were things that should remain beyond the gaze of men. This came as a considerable surprise to them.

"What, then, do you suggest, O prince?" one of the sages said on behalf of all those present as they sat on divans in 'The Double House of Life.'

"That we each play a game of draughts with the darker aspect of ourselves," replied Setnau. "I mean, dear friends, we should attempt to overcome the conceit that engenders our desire to want to know too much. Above all, let us acknowledge that our bodies are always proximate with words. When the two part—that is, when we think only in concepts, then do we find ourselves dismissing the mystery of the book."

The sages nodded their approval of this injunction. From hereon, they told themselves, the magical book and its contents must forever remain beside the coffin of Ptah-nefer-ka, so that death and the word might continue their conversation together, alone and unaided, a dialogue of inimitable grace.

A Face in the Stone

𝔉riar Francus encountered many strange things on his journey to the Orient. Once he was a guest of a Tartar prince in the province of Mancy. The dignitary lived in a palace surrounded by a wall two miles in circumference. Each alternate street inside the palace was paved in gold and silver plate. Fifty virgins attended the prince at table and fed him sweet-meats, much as birds do their young. While they placed delicate morsels between his lips the young women sang to him. The prince passed his days in a cocoon of pleasure, his fingernails growing ever longer, recreation it seems his sole respite. Only he knew the limitations of his body in relation to the realization of bliss.

After remaining in the company of the prince for some days, and watching the man deport himself in a manner befitting someone who was only half awake, Francus traveled eastward through a land of fire and ashes. At one point he heard a great noise in the air, an outcry, as if a multitude of spirits were in revolt against their gods. In a bid to escape the onslaught he retreated into a valley to wait out this concatenation of spirits, which he firmly believed was the result of a war in heaven. It was there, however, while he sat by a swift-flowing river contending with his thoughts, that he was confronted by a vision without equal in all his travels.

On the slopes of the valley, and in the vicinity of the river, Francus suddenly recognized a host of dead bodies from which sweet harmonies emanated, accompanied by music played on zithers. His curiosity aroused, and overcoming his fear of what he saw, Francus made the sign of the cross and proceeded deeper into the valley. He could not believe so many people had entered this valley of their own free will, only to fall victim to some invisible and indescribable assassin. The fact was that none of the bodies had yet entered into a stage of putrefaction. They lay about in various unlikely postures, as if each had died from a disease brought on by the extremity of their actions. Their eyes vacant, like those on ancient statues, the corpses seemed to be enacting a mummer's play, a ridiculous ceremony dedicated to the exaggerations and malefactions of the living. Francus sensed that he had stumbled into the Valley of Death.

Pressing forward, the good friar came upon a large stone on the floor of the valley on which he saw the face of a man staring at him. He was taken aback by this monstrous apparition, which reminded him of certain gargoyles, a gorgon perhaps, that he had seen on cathedrals at home in Europe. They too gazed down at him with a look that was both distorted and aggrieved. The dead, it seemed, wanted to leer at the living in a way that intimated their ultimate displeasure. They appeared to be saying that no one, not evening a pious prelate, would hope to escape putrefaction and the slow desuetude of his being. No wonder the spirits of the dead wished to revolt against the gods: they were left powerless, disembodied, and burdened with a shade's transparency in order that the gods might be free to assert their superiority. Trembling before this face in the stone as it stared lasciviously back at him, Francus concluded that all men were little more than sacrificial lambs. Birth was the wound they carried about with them even as they struggled to remain innocent.

"My realm is one where lifelessness merely pretends to be dead," the face of the gorgon spoke for the first time, its voice heavy with an air of lassitude and the agelessness of stone. "The truth is, when the senses are sated, life becomes an act of somnolence. We become dead to our bodies, with decay no more than an insipient disorder that eats away at our very being. We die not from age, but from the corruption we engender in our souls. Death is the last refuge that we seek in order to alleviate such anguish."

Francus renewed his genuflections in an attempt to overcome the shock at what he had heard. The face in the stone had delivered its own iniquitous sermon, its paean to death. All he could think of at this point was the Tartar prince living in luxury, surrounded by fifty virgins, with whom he had spent time as a guest. In his mind he was already fleeing from this valley filled with corpses along roads paved with gold and silver plate. There was no end to the emptiness, the filth, and the excrement of men bent upon consuming what they did not need. About him he could see bodies that were testimony to this excess. The entire valley was buried in the unwanted flesh of the living that had only known death in life.

Francus turned and fled from the valley. Behind him, he could hear the wailing of spirits voicing their unhappiness with their gods. He could hear also the sound of zithers playing as if in sympathy with the dead. The sight of men frozen in postures that reminded him of his own malady made him feel quite ill. Yet he secretly knew that in him a Tartar prince continued to live on, under the constant eye of virgins, half asleep to the world. More than anything he realized that the Valley of Death was a place where everyone was content to live out their lives, even as they adopted postures to camouflage what they had lost.

Interlude in a Temple

One day, in the kingdom of Mobar, Friar Francus found himself attending the annual pilgrimage of its god as a special guest of the king. His first sight of the god's image inside the temple reminded him of Saint Christopher, the patron saint of travelers. The figure also alluded to the image of Lord Shiva, himself the guardian of travelers, as well as a dancer and keeper of endless time. The god stood in a temple made from beaten gold, his image covered from head to toe in silk riband and precious stones. To Francus's untutored eye the figure in no way reflected divine life-energy as he had been led to expect by his host. Rather, all he could see was an image bedecked in oriental extravagance. As far as the good friar was concerned, the outward had overwhelmed the inward and made oblivion its pretext.

Nonetheless, out of courtesy to his host, he remained by the roadside and watched the pilgrims pass by on their way to the temple. Men with halters around their necks, others with knives buried up to the hilt in their arms, constituted the condition of many of the pilgrims who passed him on the road. Frenzied singers and acolytes beating their chests also accompanied the procession as it made its way towards a sacred lake near the temple. Here, the good friar was astounded to see many of the populace throw gold, silver and precious stones into the water before they approached. This, he was told, was payment to Lord Shiva.

The king and queen then appeared, surrounded by a multitude. The pilgrims assembled and entered the temple. Re-emerging, they triumphantly bore the image of the god on their shoulders towards a flower-bedecked chariot drawn by bulls. They placed it on the chariot; and, to the sound of music accompanied by dancers emulating the god, the procession moved off at a steady pace. As it did so, many young men deliberately threw themselves under the wheels of the chariot, and were crushed to death by the weight of the statue.

Francus could hardly conceal his dismay: after all, he had never witnessed martyrdom before. He realized that this so-called god demanded much more from its followers than a simple prayer or Hail Mary. For these people death was a most blissful experience given, that it has been offered freely and with dispassion. Feeling somewhat guilty at his eagerness to censure others for their excess, the good friar recalled that only the Lord Jesus had made such a gift in the past.

Later, when smoke from funeral pyres clouded the air in a way that made breathing difficult, Francus found himself swept along by the crowd to another ceremony near the lake. Here numerous families had gathered to conduct a feast in preparation for yet another act of self-mutilation. This time sharp knives were hung about the necks of the would-be martyrs. Young men, presumably in a state of trance induced by some opiate, suddenly climbed to their feet and cried out to the Lord Shiva. Then they cut into their flesh, severing limbs, fingers and toes in order that they might be placed as offerings on the altar of the god. Slowly, piece-by-piece, the young acolytes reduced themselves to little more than bloody torsos, each wound they inflicted upon themselves a testimony to their love of Lord Shiva and their indifference towards death. Their behavior struck Francus as the very height of madness. Almost without knowing it, he had been made witness to man's capacity for diminution taken to its logical extreme, and he didn't like what he saw.

"I yield myself to death on behalf of Lord Shiva," each man cried out as he slowly bled to death. "I am the only one, the sole survivor of this world. Now I am about to enter into a new incarnation."

Francus was severely shaken by these remarks. A part of him wished that they hadn't been translated at all. Can a man hope to renew his compact with life simply by offering it up to a god? The idea sounded preposterous. As far as he was concerned, there was a singularity about existence that precluded having a second bite of the cherry. Not even Jesus Christ had promised such a gift, unless it was his desire to bestow eternal life on all who chose to give up theirs in His name. But another incarnation—did it not suggested a multiple life, a life detached from the present one, one indeed that was forever undergoing transformation? In spite of his unease Francus felt himself drawn to this idea. The freedom from constraint implied by such a problematic condition engendered in him a growing sense of elation.

Eternity and Time was the paradox at the heart of Lord Shiva's demand upon his followers, it seemed. He wanted them to release themselves from the carapace of the here-and-now by an act of supreme self-abandonment. Giving up one's life was to counteract the demands of Time, thus allowing for the gradual process of aging and death to be neutralized. A man, in this case a martyr, took it upon himself to embrace death by cutting himself into little pieces so that each piece of his body might carry forth the minutiae of his own death to the world. In a sense—and it struck the good friar with considerable force—diminution of the body held out the possibility that a man could become like seed placed in the earth. Each aspect of himself could sprout, bloom, and wither once more. This in turn allowed for a multiplying of his personality to the power of infinity. Every man became all men—an absolute, phenomenal, and self-immortal being that was both perishable and quintessentially the same. Henceforward his personality would be able to give up duality as the last bastion of the ignorant.

Francus struggled to maintain his composure as he made his way back to his quarters in the king's compound. The sight of so many men run over by a chariot, or cut to pieces by their own hand, had left him feeling not a little squeamish. He still couldn't quite accept that there might be some cosmic significance to be found in the process of acting out so much death and mutilation in the name of a god. It didn't seem real to him.

Yet, in a strange way, he was beginning to understand. The Lord Shiva, covered in ribands of Time and Eternity, found himself impervious to these acts of disintegration. What bound him to his followers were his tranquility, his inexpressive countenance, and his imperishable nature. The god had become a transforming power who regarded destruction and regeneration as being one and the same. The good friar decided that Saint Christopher and Lord Shiva were, together, true dancers. For them the temporal was able to merge with the infinite, and so guide men to their final destination.

The Elixir of Life

$\mathcal{A}$ Portuguese merchant, recently arrived in Goa, found himself wandering aimlessly in the bazaar one day. He had completed his business transactions with the local nabob, and was now waiting for his ship to set sail. His voyage had been a profitable one; he had managed to sell his goods prior to purchasing a cargo of cloves, nutmeg, and pepper from a Malaccan trader. This he hoped to sell at a considerable profit in Lisbon on his return.

Since his ship was not due to depart for a day or so, the merchant decided to spend a little time in the bazaar in the hope of picking up an object of some antiquarian value. Without realizing it at first, he drifted into what appeared to be a bookshop, though the books themselves were printed on wafers of bamboo held together by a piece of string that passed through the center of each of these story boards.

The bookseller tried to interest him in a partly illustrated story from the Mahabharata, which he declined on the grounds that it was a pagan text. After peering at a number of other documents, the merchant's eye was finally arrested by a bamboo book that revealed a number of tiny pictures of elephants interspersed among lines of pagan script. He asked the bookseller what might be the subject of this book, to which the man replied in a quiet tone, "Elephants, *me' sahib*. And, of course, the secret to eternal life."

His curiosity aroused, the merchant agreed to purchase the document for the sum of two Venetian ducats. But on one condition—that the bookseller provide him with a translator so that the document might be transcribed into Portuguese, before he set sail for Lisbon. As the merchant planned to sell the object to an antiquarian in that fair city, he thought it might help if its subject was translated for the benefit of any prospective purchaser. The bookseller readily agreed to send a scholar to his inn early the next morning, someone who was familiar with the Portuguese language, in order to make the necessary translation.

"Make sure that he brings with him parchment and sufficient quantity of nibs," the merchant added, presenting the bookseller with two Venetian ducats.

The following morning the scholar arrived at the merchant's inn. Soon the man was seated by the open window with a view of the port beyond, his nibs set up in a stand on the desk. With their feathers neatly combed, they looked like ships' masts with sails furled riding at anchor. Patiently, and with occasional prompting from the merchant who agreed to help with those Portuguese words that eluded him, the scholar was able to render a passable copy of this rare document.

Treatise on the Elephant

The elephant is the largest of all four-footed beasts. He has ankles in the lower part of his legs, and five undivided toes on his feet. His snout or trunk is so long, and in such a remarkable serpentine form, that he is able to use it instead of a hand. With it he is able to eat and drink by bringing his trunk to his mouth. He is also able to raise his keeper onto his back and uproot trees.

Besides two great tusks, he has on either side of his mouth four teeth with which he masticates his food. The tusks of the male are greater than those of a female. It is said that when he has seasoned the female, he never after touches her. The male lives upward of one hundred and twenty years; the female, three score. They love rivers, hate the cold, and are never adulterous.

If they happen to meet a man abroad, they will immediately go before him and show him the way home. Though brave in battle, they show much respect for the wounded, which they carry away from the mêlée on their backs. It is said that they can be tamed with the juice of barley.

The scholar worked all day and into the night. He noted down the different kinds of elephants, their average height and color, and details pertaining to their skin, ears, and the much-prized quality of their tusks. By dawn, though suffering from fatigue, he was still carefully rendering each word on parchment as if it were an ornament of high artistic merit:

Elephants are continually at war against dragons, which desire to drink of their blood because it is very cold. To catch an elephant, a dragon must lie in wait for an elephant to pass. With the aid of its exceedingly long tail the dragon encircles the pachyderm's hind legs and arrests him in his tracks. Then the dragon thrusts his fire-breathing head into the elephant's trunk, causing the animal to feel faint by drawing upon its blood.

At this point the elephant tumbles to earth, crushing the dragon as it falls. The dragon is split open, pouring forth the elephant's blood and its own onto the ground. In this way the cold blood of the elephant mingles with the hot blood of the dragon to form cinnabar, or Dragon's Blood.

This, according to the sages of old, is none other than the sacred elixir of immortal life. One draught of Dragon's Blood will grant a man courage to give up his death-seeking occupations in the hope of attaining to a state where age is of little consequence. Any man that partakes of the eternity of elephants, which is none other than the ethereal breath of cinnabar, will find himself forever beholden to these gentle beasts.

Although it was late in the morning when the scholar completed his task, it seemed like an age had passed. To the weary merchant, who had fallen asleep hours earlier and had only just now awoken, the revelation of these remarkable insights pertaining to the power of Dragon's Blood came as a surprise. Clearly this ancient pagan text had tapped into a rich vein of occult knowledge. The merchant realized at once that he had become the keeper of eternal life even if his original motive had been one of profit. How could he sell such an item, he asked himself? How could he pass onto an antiquarian in Lisbon the secret of eternal life for the sum of a few seraphins of gold? It didn't seem right.

"You are aware," the scholar remarked, as he put down his last nib and rubbed his bloodshot eyes, "that this document is at once a danger and revelation to the world. It is a fact that some sentences release both their poison and their curative properties only after long years lying at rest in a discarded book. We now know that elephants, wise creatures that they are, carry within them the secret of eternal life. Are we not therefore as dragons, sucking forth their blood so that we might partake of their untimely existence?"

Believing the scholar to be speaking in riddles, the merchant nonetheless nodded his head in agreement. Talk of Dragon's Blood as cinnabar, of mythical creatures gorging on elephant's blood in the name of eternal life, such remarks struck him as the makings of a conceit for which the East was renowned. The world could do without confabulation, he decided. But, even as the scholar duly presented him with the bundle of parchment pages covered in words, bowed before him, and then gathered up his writing materials in readiness to depart, he decided to ask him one last question.

"Is it true," he demanded, "that an elephant's tusk is the product of age, or perhaps some other extreme act of comportment?"

"Both," the scholar replied, as he stuffed his worn nibs into a satchel. "In its death struggle with a dragon, the elephant relies on its memory of past encounters. There is a long history of bloodlines commingling in such extreme gestures of pathos. Sympathy, you see, is essential to the realization of consanguinity. Eternal life, and therefore the probable length of an elephant's tusk, can only be the result of a certain temerity shown in regard to its decision to merge with another. Alone among creatures, the elephant and dragon are blood brothers. They seek to express their lives as cinnabar, as none other than what is known as the "vermilion of eternal life," rather than remain committed to the contingency of individual forms. It is this that makes the elephant's tusk such an object of value for men like us, for it alone represents the congealed breath of the dragon merging with the unusual bulk of the pachyderm. We cherish the beauty of such a union of opposites, do we not? Making temperate what is hot and cold blood is another way, I suspect, of creating the smooth consistency of ivory."

Later, when the scholar had taken his leave, the merchant stood at the window gazing at the flotilla of ships riding at anchor in the harbor beyond. His caravel, he knew, was out there somewhere, its hull sunk low in the water. On the tide later that day it was to sail back to the Old World, along with its precious cargo.

It dawned on him then that his ship was about to transport an object of even greater worth than spices or elephant tusks. The *Treatise on the Elephant,* with its secret formula for the elixir of life, would surely protect him from monsoon winds or pirates on the long voyage home. Then again, if it didn't, it might even provide him with something he hadn't bargained for: a voyage to an unknown land where dragons and elephants continue to engage in eternal combat so that their blood might intermingle, making it possible for immortal life to settle and congeal in the residue left over from such a battle. Cinnabar, he knew, would from henceforth remain his favorite color, as well as the instrument of his survival.

A Singular Man

"I have searched myself"
—Heraclitus

*T*omas Gerhardt lived in an apartment overlooking the river in downtown Zurich. He had spent much of his life surrounded by books, which of course he devoured with passionate interest. His only other pastime was to play the harpsichord in his library late at night, savoring each note as it was plucked. Strains of Scarlatti often permeated the stairwell leading to the bank offices below. Long-time employees of the bank confided among themselves that music and money were not altogether incompatible; each, in its own way, was music to the ear. The man playing in his library above had inadvertently alerted them to the existence of invisible chords that governed the orchestration of wealth.

Gerhardt's apartment was a strange combination of austere decoration and opulence. On the wall of the living-room a priceless medieval tapestry depicted the Marriage of Cana, while on a plinth in one corner stood an African burial mask. A witch-doctor's rattle made of bones lay in a tray on the coffee table next to a large, ornately bound book depicting hieroglyphs from the Tomb of Rameses in Luxor. To say that his tastes were eclectic was to demean their effect: his life, it seems, was governed more by disparity than any desire to titillate his senses. Gerhardt's world had come to rest amid things that bore a remarkable likeness to the primordial nature of his psyche. He had turned his mind into a museum.

To attain stillness was his objective. Once, in a Greek Psalter from his library, he had come across the word *apatheia*, which meant the same thing. To Gerhardt, apathy seemed like a worthy condition to want to achieve since it implied a distancing from the normal contingencies of existence. He longed to remain neutral, without attachments, a living chromosome yet to realize its true identity and function in life. He saw himself not as man in a bespoke suit who happened to step out with an umbrella on his arm (whether it looked like it might rain or not), but as someone in league with light. Fearful of encountering untoward radiance during the course of his day, nonetheless over time he had learnt to carry a small measure of it about on his person. In moments of self-deprecation, however, Gerhardt often remarked to himself that, though he may well see himself as "illuminated," someone had accidentally switched off his light!

This was the man who one morning decided to catch the night train to Florence. It was not a decision taken on the spur of the moment so much as one inspired by a curious need. For some time he had felt a strong desire to view one of Michelangelo's sculptures of a slave bunched and stooped under the cruel weight of stone on its back. The caryatid was housed in a museum opposite the Duomo, along with a number of other Florentine masterpieces rescued from the rubble of the past. The slave, he decided, depicted an aspect of himself. He wanted to see what it was like to be burdened by the sufferings of the world.

More importantly, Gerhardt told himself, he wanted to understand the precise nature of that stone on the caryatid's shoulders—indeed, to question its very substance. Was it made up of chords from a Scarlatti sonata or the bones of a witch-doctor's rattle? To put it more succinctly, was the stone a manifestation of beauty or ugliness? Could the world's suffering be the result of an unbridgeable division in the psyche of everyone, including himself? These questions filled his thoughts. In a very real sense Gerhardt saw himself standing at the bottom of a chasm into which light rarely penetrated, except when the sun was at its zenith. Of all the people he knew (which wasn't many), he alone felt that he had a responsibility to relieve the slave of its burden.

Arriving in Florence the following morning, he took a taxi to his hotel on a side street leading to the Duomo. The marble facade of the cathedral rose dramatically before him with all the tonalities of coral. For a moment he thought of himself diving over a reef, so exquisite were the schools of gargoyles and sculptural reliefs depicted on the upper walls. He imagined himself awash in all the aquatic excrescence of the Tropics. Each image before him was like a fish plucked as a note on his harpsichord. The Duomo became a lagoon in which myriads of creatures swam slowly past. Re-assured as to his vocation as a diver, Gerhardt crossed the square and entered the museum.

The rooms and corridors were filled with fragments of stone, medieval sculpture from the Duomo, an altarpiece encircled by a relief depicting a choir in the company of musicians, and a model of the cathedral dome prepared by its original architect. Gerhardt's initial impression of the museum was one of confusion; there was no clear theme to the exhibit other than that of a trail of wayward stone longing to find a more permanent home. He began to ask himself why it was that men carved certain images, only to find them discarded by a later age. It was then that he recognized his own penchant for playing the occasional chord too rapidly on his harpsichord back home. Impatience with the familiar often bred in one a mild contempt, he realized.

Eventually Gerhardt arrived in the central courtyard of the museum. Light streamed through the glass roof above, giving the illusion of eternal sunlight. In a fleeting moment he imagined himself on that tropical beach where he had seen skeletons of crustaceans and empty sea-shells. But standing there before him, like an abandoned sand castle at low tide, stood Michelangelo's caryatid bearing an infinite load on its shoulders. He was taken aback. He was aghast. No one had predicted that such an image of servitude could begin to evoke in him such a deep antipathy towards the idea that man imposed his own level of inhumanity upon himself. It seemed that he had become a victim of his own actions even as he wielded a whip over others.

Dazed, Tomas Gerhardt continued to gaze at the statue, his state verging upon incredulity. How could a block of stone, a conglomerate of matter no less, embody such a confused mass of emotions? Did Michelangelo sense what it was like to bear the burden of the world on his shoulders? Of course he must have, given the way in which he had carved the slave with his unbearable load. It was almost as if a man needed to stoop low under the weight of failure in order to honor what is intrinsic about his character.

Then it dawned upon Gerhardt what this quality might be. It was to do with light and certain chords in a Scarlatti sonata. It was to do with an understanding of what *apatheia* might mean as it drifted through one's being as an obscure yet living chromosome. Stillness, he realized, was the essential character of Christ in Cana that day, when he managed to turn water into wine. Was it not true that he had transformed ordinary reality into something of a more elevated nature, thus giving new meaning to the idea of marriage? Of course! The contents of that stone in the guise of a caryatid were the very ingredients of life. They were the tiny, everyday irritants that rubbed against themselves to produce either beauty or ugliness, depending on whether one wished to celebrate a communion or not.

Tomas Gerhardt left the museum in a state of high spirits. The caryatid had worked its magic. Bearing his own silent burden, he crossed the piazza in front of the Duomo, noticing with pleasure that its façade was already awash in sunlight. The ocean that was this cathedral had all but drowned him in its interminable current of fabulous effects. The gargoyles and sculptural reliefs above him were now as plankton spreading their invisible nutrient across the sea of his heart. He was a whale now, a leviathan swimming towards warmer waters.

An Urban Ascetic

If there was any creature that Tomas Gerhardt felt a secret kinship with, then it was the sole. He liked the fact that its mouth and eyes were on the same side of its body, and that it was able to submerge in the sand whenever danger threatened. These characteristics suggested adaptability, as well as a desire to remain unnoticed. He was more than conscious that, if a man was to grace the world in a spirit of singular inquiry, it was incumbent on him to adopt some form of camouflage. The sole was the ideal model. This fish's elongated, some might say *squashed* appearance, made survival its primary imperative. Gerhardt knew that to make the sea-floor into its watery haven a sole had to first perfect the art of abasement. For a man like himself it was of considerable comfort to know that nature had defined nobility in terms of a boldly realized disfigurement.

Nor was it true that Gerhardt allowed himself to contract when confronted with normal life. Far from it. He readily admitted to himself, however, that there were limits to the way he embraced all its facets. He knew, for example, that he could not remain "with it" for very long, if only because of his commitment to things and events of a more untimely nature. He would always be more in tune with a line of Villon's poetry than that of a football result in last Saturday's club match. If he possessed a dream, then it was to "float on life" like certain insects that are capable of walking on water. He saw himself as a man in league with circumstance, with uncertainty, and with the wider workings of the cosmos.

Gerhardt read passable Latin but no Greek. He dabbled in astrology and wrote the occasional poem in English—not, as one might expect, in his native German. A widower of some years, he looked back at his marriage to a woman of Gaelic origin with fondness. She had monitored his engagement with the world in a way that he might have found impossible otherwise. If he had experienced any intimacy with ladies celebrated for their beauty during those years, it was always with the knowledge that his wife sanctioned his actions with, if not understanding, then acceptance. Their marriage, he recalled, had been one of secrecy that blossomed during moments of seasonal exuberance.

On the death of his wife, Tomas Gerhardt had decided to compact his life. Gone were the large house in town, the country estate, the cars, the overseas holidays and wine cellar. In their place was a small wardrobe consisting of a couple of suits, two panama hats, a pair of hiking boots for walking in the Alps, a silk scarf for evening wear, and a selection of tailored shirts that he always purchased from a shop near the Rialto in Venice. His new mode of life – its *slimness*, so to speak – gave him a sense of freedom he had not known previously.

If there was any one thing about modern life that disconcerted him, however, it was the idea of mechanism. More and more, it seemed, everything he did was conditioned by the press of a button. He longed for a time, in his youth, when the prospect of building something—a cart or a balsa aeroplane, for example—was something one actually set out to do rather than purchase ready-made. He believed that a quality inherent in "handiwork" had been lost as soon as others became responsible for creating whatever one desired. For him, the act of construction had always been very personal, if only because it signified a renewed attachment to the sanctity of things.

Indeed, Tomas Gerhardt readily admitted to himself that "disjointedness" was a symptom of life. Of course he preferred the Greek word for it, even though for him it was a crib. "Anachronistic" seemed such a beautiful word. When he broke it down into parts he immediately recognized its link with Chronos, the ancient god of Time. To be out of kilter with time suggested to him a fluid condition, something akin to oil in an amphora aboard a merchant ship bound for Rhodes.

Why Rhodes? Because he immediately associated the island with the Colossus standing on a headland at the entrance to its port, a figure he knew had enjoyed a brief holiday from the depredations of age until an earthquake finally claimed it. That which was "disjointed" was thus precariously positioned on the edge of the sea gazing towards openness, towards a promise as yet unrealized. This bird of passage he likened to a swallow forever grappling with all the suscitations of air.

In his later years the world had begun to embrace him with a certain ease. He did not know whether this was as a result of the accommodation that he had reached with his past, or whether he had entered into a new relationship with the present. Either way, he now recognized the worth of what he considered to be his life-long affliction, this weighing-up of contingencies and acceptance of the principle of incertitude. Being out of kilter with the world reminded him of a canoe negotiating rapids.

Tomas Gerhardt had attained to a state of what he liked to think of as foam. Whether wandering the back streets of Paris or Rome, he was conscious that the whole world seemed to bubble. Equilibrium, for him, implied a genuine harmony between himself and the world. Though it might be a momentary condition, he had learned to recognize its symptoms. Like the sole that takes on the color of sand, and flattens its body so that it becomes invisible, Gerhardt could feel himself doing the same.

This became more evident to him when he stepped out onto his small roof-top terrace above the river in his city in order to breathe in the morning air. A wild duck from the lake had chosen to lay its eggs among the pot plants four floors up from the river, and away from urban predators. That morning he was suddenly confronted by half a dozen ducklings scrambling about in the gutters in readiness for their departure. Their featherless bodies looked fragile and incomplete. How would they get down, he mused? How will they reach the river? Surely they would plummet to the sidewalk and be killed. Gerhardt prepared himself for their lemming-like leap into the void.

Suddenly the female duck glided from the roof to the pavement below. There she stood and waited. In rapid order the six ducklings followed suit. Each in turn leapt out into the abyss and slowly spiraled, like dandelions on a spring day, towards the pavement. Gerhardt was amazed. He had never seen anything like it before. Nature had devised a way for these creatures to float through the air! They were weightless.

Without at first realizing it, Tomas Gerhardt turned the gesture back on himself. He began to see himself as one of these ducklings, floating earthwards, a creature of infinite lightness. How can it be, he asked himself? After a lifetime, it seems, I am able to—yes, to float on air! I am a bubble adrift, foam on the breeze, inconsequential yet strangely significant, if only to myself. I have put my trust in those lasting amplitudes that masquerade as forces of nature—forces that in the past I might have regarded as acts of disfigurement. In reality, they are more akin to the subtle art of abasement, a quality that he identified with the sole.

A car stopped below. The duck and her brood waddled across the road, mounted the curb, and leapt into the river where they embraced for the first time a new medium, that of water. Ah, Gerhardt thought, this delight in incertitude, this embrace of the indefinable. We are all mere ducklings bare of feathers, preparing to leap into the abyss. We are all Time's children, waddling towards depredation and age. But before we do, let's put on a clean shirt, a panama hat, and step out into the sunlight—and become, in the process, a Colossus upon a headland.

Where Less is More

For some time Tomas Gerhardt had been giving consideration to his own demise. Death, it seemed, had crept up on him with all the patience of a cat stalking a bird. It might assert itself in the sound of water over riverstones, or in a lark's cry at dusk. However much he thought about it—his inertness, the placid nature of his remains lying in a morgue—he always tried to at least invent an image to carry the moment of his cessation beyond the reach of either grave or crematorium. I lie in the cusp of a grinding stone, he mused, one that is worn smooth by generations of tribeswomen grinding out seed for her family. Ah yes, I am little more than a husk. Then he would smile, content to know that he had discovered something solid to cosset his bones.

Such thoughts made him realize the fragility of life. All the exertion and will required to survive was as if nothing when compared to the inevitable destruction of flesh once the spirit had chosen to make its exit. Stage left, he thought. Muted applause. Then everyone leaves the theatre to be overwhelmed once more by their habitual concerns. The play has become a part of memory for them. On the other hand I, the leading actor, am left to remove my makeup and so disappear. All performances are transitory, Gerhardt realized, racked by the disease of time.

Unless . . .

It was this "unless" that returned time and again to engage his thoughts. It was like the angel wrestling with Jacob at the foot of a ladder as he attempted to ascend. To where, Gerhardt asked himself? He was no Jack climbing the beanstalk in order to confront a giant. These images from mythology did little to satisfy his wish to delve more deeply into the exact condition this word might actually reflect. When dismembered (a word suitably appropriate to his present musings), "unless" implied something that was *less* than less! It suggested the faded imprint of a fern leaf in stone, a petroglyph of incomparable age and delicacy.

So there it was. Daily he went about his business with the word suppurating in his thoughts. It was like a Japanese *koan* promising so much in the way of revelation, if only he could unlock its meaning. That it was no Sound of One Hand Clapping, he acknowledged. Yet at another level he knew that the lessness of less was rich in connotations. He began to see it as the labyrinth into which Theseus had plunged in order to defeat the Minotaur. Down those dark passageways of lessness he wandered towards the lair of the beast, knowing that in some way he was protected. The beautiful Ariadne, after all, had provided him with enough thread to lead him back to the world.

Yet this idea only partly satisfied him. If lessness was no more than a confused network of passageways, and not the ultimate object of his quest, then what lay beyond? He had no clue. Experience told him, however, that if minimalism could be considered as a journey without end, then surely lessness had something to do with a pilgrimage. Gerhardt thought at once of Canterbury, of Santiago de Compostela in Spain, even Jerusalem at the time of the Crusades. These were places that clearly embodied the obverse of the Minotaur's cave. They were home to a sense of an objective attained, of a lasting repose. If "unless" implied the embodiment of what is minimal, and the journey upon which it was based found its natural rhythm in the idea of being forever "on the road," then surely there was a thread that bound them. Again the likes of Ariadne must have something to do with it, he decided.

Sitting on top of his rooftop terrace overlooking the river, with spring sunshine greening the trees on the street below, and outdoor tables already cluttering the pavement in the old city on the far bank, Tomas Gerhardt pondered how far his thoughts had departed from his initial meditation upon death. Aloneness, if that could be construed as a state of mind, had invaded his thoughts. He felt it seep into the narrowest crevasses of his mind. Moreover, it glittered like salmon leaping over rapids. It too was a part of "unless" as it pursued its journey upriver towards those spawning grounds. There, he thought! We are drawn towards a place where renewal is orchestrated, where the heart is fertilized by the overleaping energy and exuberance that comes from birth.

So "aloneness" and "unless" are linked by an overleaping energy, he thought. Now he really did feel as if he were swimming out into deeper water. Should he turn back? Something was luring him onward, a siren perhaps, whose voice was keening an exquisite dirge. Like Theseus he must move forward, trusting his instincts to protect him if he were to escape the Labyrinth. If solitude, and finding oneself minus everything, were the primary condition of death, then surely there was a lesson in that. It may be, he argued with himself, that the heart yearns to reach a state that lies beyond such limitations.

Still, Gerhardt was unconvinced. Something told him that he had become entangled in words. He had made these more important than what they embodied. Bandying about "unless," "aloneness," "pilgrimage," "lessness" as well as "Japanese *koans*" may well have taken him on a voyage, but still he was nowhere nearer his destination. There was something empty in the emptiness of words, he told himself. They too were gouged out like a grinding stone awaiting a deposit of grain. Or was it bones?

Below, people hurried along the pavement or sat in cafés to take coffee and read the morning newspaper. They could be maggots, he told himself, consuming the body politic before his very eyes. No, that's stupid: they are salmon swimming upstream to their spawning grounds. Without realizing it, Tomas Gerhardt was embroiled in the business of detaching himself from life. He was beginning to lose all sense of himself. Everything he observed was suddenly transformed into another set of images altogether. This, he told himself, is the way death creeps up on a man unawares. To die, then, is to dismantle the world.

Gerhardt leant on the railing and gazed out across the lake and the city. Clearly he had the best of both worlds. On the one hand he lived above it all; on the other, he could see it as it was—a shifting panoply of moods as each season asserted its rights and prerogatives over the earth. So it's true, he remarked to himself: my death is but a crow perched upon a leafless bough on an autumn evening. It is a sentinel entrusted to watch over my passing.

Then he recalled Anubis, the jackal-headed god of the ancient Egyptians standing at the entrance to the realm of Tuat, the Underworld. Now that's an image, he thought. A dog overseeing death! Surrounded by crows and dogs, it now seemed that Gerhardt had entered into a colloquium with animals in a bid to come to terms with his departure from the world. If they happened to caw or growl, it only meant that the language of death was less one of words than it was of utterance. Physical and mental annihilation were tied up with a whole menagerie of feelings by which the spirit quietly made peace with all the travails of existence.

Suddenly he recalled the thread that Ariadne had provided Theseus with in order to lead him safely out of the Labyrinth. Of course this ploy had saved him from remaining imprisoned in the Minotaur's cave. To cut the thread, however, implied the inconsolable grief of death, rather than the connubiality between it and life. Cutting the thread, Gerhardt realized, was to transcend this relativity. Without death there could be no life. Flames would not flare and dance without wood burning down to ashes. What survived this connubiality was the knowledge that the principle of combustion remained eternal. In the same way, Gerhardt told himself (and with some relief), men live and die, but the flame of human existence burns forever.

Below, in the river, the ducks that had recently survived their fall through space drifted past, an aquatic echelon of contentment. To this man living in his eerie above the bank, this fledgling that had yet to test his wings, knowing that he had cut the thread leading him out of the cave that housed his rather confused thoughts on death, relieved him of some of his concerns. Anubis is watching over me, he thought. In the theater of life, it seems that I am yet to perform my most dramatic role.

The Bust of Nefertiti

Of all the women that Tomas Gerhardt had desired in his life, none were more alluring than those that he had encountered in various art galleries thoughout the world. The *Naked Maya* by Goya in Madrid, the *Rokeby Venus* by Velasquez in London, and Ingres's *Grande Odalisque* in Paris, through these women he had managed to fashion what he considered to be his ideal of the Perfect Woman. Such attributes were both tactile and subjective: each quality of the feminine he regarded as a coalescence between mind and matter. The Perfect Woman embodied intelligence, charm, elegance, exquisite delicacy, and a yearning for those pleasures that the body offered. Thus the Naked Maya invited, the Rokeby Venus tantalized, and Ingres' Grande Odalisque intimated a perfect sensuality. All three women, though admittedly the product of these artists' imaginations, remonstrated with his own; and so their painterly life transcended the solitude of their imaginary existence.

On a trip to Egypt one year to study hieroglyphs in the tombs outside Luxor, Gerhardt did what most tourists do: he purchased a small alabaster copy from a roadside stall of the bust of Nefertiti discovered among the excavations at Tel Amarna. It was a well executed sculpture, retaining many of the qualities of stillness that he had witnessed in the original in Berlin some years before. Her regal nature was plain to see. Nefertiti imparted a deep sympathy with distance, suffering, and the many responsibilities that come with ruling a kingdom. Hers had been a life dedicated to service and the aspirations of a man bent upon introducing a new spiritual dimension to the world. This man was none other than her husband, the Pharaoh Akhenaton.

Some days later, when he had taken a room at the Old Cataract Hotel in Aswan overlooking the Nile in order to enjoy a few days rest from his travels, Gerhardt pondered the antiquity of his new acquisition as it lay before him on the table. The mere thought of the bust of Nefertiti lying among rubble for thousands of years (such a frozen and perfect image of beauty, he thought) provoked him to consider its implications. We build up certain pictures, he told himself—pictures that only serve to confirm our view of reality as representing an unchanging event, a certitude. Nefertiti's beauty has transcended time. She reaches out to us from beyond the grave, touching us immeasurably. Her reality is one of intractable grace married to that of imperial order. Yet the subsequent demise of the Egyptian civilization has not erased such an image from our minds. She simply is, he thought.

"So there's an isness about certain things," he announced, as he gazed at the ruins of a temple across the water, above a flapping felucca's sail gliding along the river. "You, madam, have made it impossible to dismiss the culmination of forms that have gone into your creation." Then he checked himself, realizing how absurd it was to be addressing a statue and not a person.

Nonetheless the thought would not go away. He had come to Egypt to study how the Egyptians had expressed their belief in lasting values. They were not a people given to skating over the surface, he realized. Their written language, too, was an amalgam of images taken from nature, which in turn expressed complex abstract ideas. Thus a line of birds, a baboon, two snakes, and a grove of papyrus reeds could be suddenly transformed into an invocation to a god or the announcement of a Pharaoh's recent military achievement. It was breathtaking: one set of realities from nature had been transformed into another, that of a people's need to record the wonder and miracle of their own ability to think.

This struck Gerhardt as pertinent. He had always lived with the belief that when men thought, they thought in words! But the Egyptians, he realized, thought in images. They thought the world as if through the prism of things. Their idea of the Perfect Woman was thus the conglomeration of creaturely attributes that were a far cry from his idea of the sensuous lines of a nude body, or a winsome smile! Nefertiti's beauty lay in her power and regality, in her submission to the eternal nature of the Pharaoh as a principle of kingship. For the Egyptians, it seemed, beauty lay not in the eyes of the beholder as he had assumed, but in the unchanging expression of a reality underscored by the proximity of death.

It began to dawn on him then that beauty and death were in some way linked. What he had initially thought of as widely differing conditions now seemed to be more like Siamese twins. They shared the same organs, so to speak—a heart or lungs perhaps. They required the same sustenance to survive. Physical beauty, at least, was nourished by an inexhaustible desire to please. While death, that sentinel whose primary condition was darkness, made age its cohort in its bid to possess beauty. One fed upon the other, he told himself, like the divine Uroborus feeding upon its own tail.

Tomas Gerhardt recalled that, like himself, the famous British mystery writer Agatha Christie had taken up residence in the Old Cataract Hotel many years before in order to write one of her most enduring novels, *Death on the Nile*. It struck him as no coincidence that Miss Christie had chosen a river so closely associated with the ritual of death to create her own more personalized vision of murder and mayhem. Could it be, he asked, that the so-called "serenity of the Nile" often spoken about by visitors masked a penchant for instability and disruption? After all, the river's annual flood was no more than a carefully orchestrated act of destruction.

Thus beauty, serenity, desire, charm and elegance—all words used to describe a condition of physical harmony and wellbeing—now found themselves mired in the black mud and swirling waters of an ancient river in flood. These were the hieroglyphs of a language that made up the ever-changing image of perfection, a state nonetheless that was both fragile and tremulous. Only in death could a person or creature, however beautiful, find repose in an unchanging condition, that of dissolution. The Naked Maya, the Rokeby Venus or the Grande Odalisque, for all the seductive beauty and elegance of these women, were as fronds of papyrus floating on the river of life, drifting downstream towards their encounter with the vast anonymity of the sea. This, Gerhardt told himself, was the final act in a pageant once known as the "Merging of the Waters." Such an event alone constituted what he now recognized as the perfect ambivalence of being.

"At any given moment," he remarked, as much to the statue of Nefertiti on the table in front of him as to the ruined temple across the water, "my body is both a hieroglyph of life and death, beauty and ugliness. I live not in the domain of perfection so much as that of transition. It seems that everything I do in life is an act of self-destruction."

So why go through with it, he asked himself? Why remain on this endless treadmill of suffering? Because it is Maya, he recalled—the Indian expression for the illusory nature of life. It is naked and alluring too, seductive and filled with pleasure, and so an endless source of transience and charm. How can I not partake of such a cornucopia and gorge upon it, even if I know that one day it will be emptied of its fruits?

Then it struck him: attaining to a state of emptiness is the beginning of a process of fulfillment. The cornucopia known as life must be plundered so that beauty and death might be enjoined.

The Wedding Ring

$\mathcal{M}$y meeting with Tomas Gerhardt was fortuitous; we were both sitting at different tables in a café on the piazza outside the Duomo di San Lorenzo in Perugia one morning, waiting patiently for a summer storm to pass over. I had come to this rather pleasant Umbrian city to view the Virgin Mary's wedding ring in one of the cathedral's chapels, reputedly held in a gilded box protected by fifteen locks. Legend relates that the ring, set with a pale gray agate, changed color in accordance with the character of whoever wore it. I was not unsympathetic to the idea that a ring might endorse the probity of a person—or indeed the reverse. It meant that inert matter, in this case a semi-precious stone, was susceptible to the idea that virtue or vice could in some measure be coaxed forth from the most secret recesses of the heart by way of human contact.

In contrast, Tomas Gerhardt was on the last day of a tour of ancient Etruscan towns around Tuscany and Umbria as part of his investigation into the origins of pre-Romanic Italy. He had just completed a visit to the local museum of antiquities when a sudden downpour had forced him to seek shelter in the café where I happened to be drinking coffee. Within a few minutes we had struck up a conversation and, perceiving that we were both interested in similar things, we deliberately allowed ourselves a little time to explore our respective obsessions. It was as if the rain had brought us together.

"It is rather strange to imagine, don't you think?" Tomas Gerhardt ventured, "that a ring of admittedly such uncertain origin as the Holy Virgin's wedding ring might possess properties capable of determining the nature of a man's character. Of course, I am aware that this assertion is probably more miraculous than real."

"I have no doubt," I replied. "However, are you not aware that agate was once highly valued as a talisman among the ancients? It was said to be capable of quenching one's thirst, as well as protecting a man from fever. Persian magicians, I understand, used agate to divert impending storms."

"How interesting. One could say that the destiny of this stone is forever linked to water. In its presence, therefore, one finds oneself either parched or fearful of drowning!"

I smiled. Tomas Gerhardt, for all his casual wit and sense of the absurd, was nonetheless willing to allude to the existence of a double meaning embodied in agate. Perhaps he wanted me to consider whether the ring's capacity to detect vice or virtue was, in fact, a metaphor for something else—one's conscience, for example, or the complex reasoning behind ethical behavior. It seemed almost inconceivable to me that a stone might retain qualities associated with values, or indeed possess any moral sense at all.

Gazing at the Fontana Maggiore through the rain in the centre of the piazza, with its carefully sculpted reliefs fashioned from pink and white marble depicting the liberal arts, as well as selected episodes from the Old Testament such as that of Adam and Eve—and also, I noticed, that of a heraldic lion, symbol of the Guelph party, which had ruled the city during the Middle Ages—I realized that stone could indeed be seen to embody certain attributes. The entire history and culture of Perugia, its aspirations and its conflicts, was as if crafted into this fountain, thereby ensuring that the memory of these events were never lost. It was ironical, to say the least, that the two bronze nymphs standing in the upper basin, from which a constant stream of water spilled over into the fountain, should have had to compete with the rain that morning. Probably they were there to remind onlookers that water and stone are inseparable companions after all.

"I do believe, *señor*," Tomas Gerhardt addressed me as if I were Italian—delighting, I suspect, in his own faltering use of a foreign language in my presence, "that we must learn to accept a certain latitude in our dealings with things. They may not lead a psychological life as we do, but nonetheless they do not exist, shall I say, in a vacuum of sensibility."

"You may, if only I knew what you mean by the term "a vacuum of sensibility," I responded.

Tomas Gerhardt nodded in the direction of the fountain, which glistened dully in the rain.

"What you see in the centre of the piazza," he added, "is clearly a marriage between stone and thought. It is as if the marble reliefs are speaking out, thereby informing us of the permanent nature of our ideals whenever they find themselves merged with the very constitution of marble. No vacuum of sensibility can possibly exist when you have such a marriage, surely."

"Are you suggesting," I asked, "that we embody certain qualities which we advertently associate with stone?"

"We are travelers, you and I," Tomas responded. "We move from one place to another in pursuit of knowledge. Do we not then begin to identify ourselves with metaphors even as we wander? Often we remark that we "gather no moss," or that we are no more than "rolling stones" as we drift between cities. In both cases we see ourselves in relation to that of the workings of natural phenomena. The objects of this world thus assume the identity of what we see as ourselves. Or perhaps the reverse is more to the point."

"Which is why the Holy Virgin's wedding ring was said to have taken upon itself all the vices or virtues that make up a part of the wearer's personality," I suggested. "In some sense the agate becomes a consummation of his or her essential character."

"As I grow older, I begin to feel I am no longer so much a sensible being," Gerhardt continued. "It is as if I am now as pebbles in a stream through which rushing water flows. I am alert to a different kind of presumption, however: that the water flowing past me has made me what I am—a channel, a concentration of energies, which, in their own way, bolster and strengthen *who* I am, if that doesn't sound like a contradiction in terms."

"Does this mean, Tomas, that your so-called psychological self has been ameliorated, its passion for identity has gone into hibernation?"

"In a manner of speaking, yes. I have become like one of those reliefs on the fountain, or as agate in the wedding ring. I absorb and reflect the myriad tonalities of anguish in the world. I am a milestone on the road to nowhere, a *herm* signifying passage but not destination. Is it not possible, *señor,* to see oneself as one huge block of marble upon which inscrutable nature has carved out a relief? I think we can. In fact, I am firmly convinced we have forgotten how to relate to the inwardness of things. This is why we no longer produce great sculptors anymore, or why we are incapable of building cathedrals like the one we see before us. To do so is to once more acknowledge the contumacy between ourselves and nature."

"I am confused," I replied. "On the one hand you argue for the acquisition of a sensibility that has gone beyond the psychological, the sensibility of stone, so to speak. Yet on the other hand you make a plea for a sensibility that is devoid of outcome. Does this make sense?"

"It does," Tomas acknowledged, "just so long as you regard it as remaining in the realm of the illogical. We are dealing here with a condition that is not so much mind-centered as it is thought-centered. There is a difference. The former is governed by reason and explanation; while the latter is moved by a keen sense of the interdependence of things and their power as images. You see, *señor,* I am a firm believer in the fact that what we imagine is the product of the inner life of objects. A tree does not think so much as it meditates. A stone, as inert as it may seem, nonetheless has the power to empathize with its environment. A land that reflects calm, as well as beauty, is a land at peace with itself. It is these qualities that we absorb imaginatively, and so make our own."

"There are clear implications in what you're saying," I remarked, noticing that the rain was beginning to ease. The fountain in the piazza seemed to be awaiting the advent of sunlight so that it could once more sparkle with all the illusion of silver.

"In what way?"

"All of us, today, find ourselves on the brink of a particular kind of despair. It is to do with our disappointment with ourselves in relation to the world. I suspect, Tomas, that we have failed its best instincts. By this I mean that, for too long we have treated it as a utility, when in reality the world is, in a mysterious sort of way, an icon."

"Because we don't see it as such, our despair becomes more acute," responded Tomas Gerhardt.

"Exactly!" I replied.

"Now you understand why I speak of myself and stone in the same breath. The language of marble is the language of earth. Its texture speaks to us. Its sculpted form graces us with its inner nature. Marble, after all, is the perfect poet!"

I gazed across the square. The sun had come out, and the fountain with its innumerable reliefs depicting medieval life shone like a beacon. In that moment it was a voice speaking out from the past, as if urging me to participate in its timeless celebration. How glad I was it had rained that morning. If it hadn't, then I would not have had the good fortune to meet Tomas Gerhardt—a man, I decided, who was as much a sculptor as a poet.

Meanwhile, Tomas Gerhardt generously paid for our coffee and rose to go.

"Remember, *señor*," he said as we shook hands. "There are but few of us left today who are able to comprehend the value of despair as an antidote to the disease associated with false hope."

"It remains to be seen whether the Holy Virgin's wedding ring could warm to such a paradox," I replied, bidding him good day.

A Talking Forest

"To speak is to fall into tautology."
—Jorge Luis Borges

I had journeyed to Kuching in Borneo at the instigation of a friend. He advised me that if I wished to broaden my investigations into the possibility that objects prefigured words as a system of visual communication, then I needed to discuss the matter with certain *lemambang*, or oral historians, living among the Iban people in the rainforest. According to him, these men possessed powers of expression far in excess of our own. Linguistically, it seems, they had discovered a method of going beyond words in their attempt to comprehend the true nature of their world.

Of course I greeted his premise with skepticism. Nonetheless, I knew that he expected me to follow up on his advice, so I flew to Borneo in the hope of proving him entirely correct in his opinion—or else returning home empty-handed. As far as I was concerned the argument was simple enough: either the Iban people had discovered a mode of communication that transcended poetry, or else the science of phonetics had been reduced to a solitary and absurd exercise in the business of conjugating sounds. Frankly, I could not imagine how a seed-pod or a shower of rain, say, could form the basis of a word, without that word pre-empting the object itself, at least in a linguistic sense.

But my friend was adamant: the *lemambang* were able to carry words in their shoulder-bags in the same way that we do objects. In the electronic age in which we live this was more than an anachronism; it was ridiculous.

"The truth is," my friend said as he bid me good-bye at the gateway to the departure lounge, "the Iban people have learnt how to distill expression to its very essence. When they speak, words become like mist which accumulates as drops of water on a leaf."

This remark struck me as being more like a Japanese *haiku* than a statement about communication. I began to suspect that my friend had succumbed to the lure of the Orient after a recent trip there. He was beginning to see objects as if they were intimately arranged in a Taoist or Zen scroll painting. They had become, in a sense, no longer determined by categories but by aesthetics.

Arriving in Kuching, I sought out a translator and guide to take me into the Borneo jungle where the Iban people lived in their longhouses, surrounded by the mutilated heads of their enemies. Since they had given up the practice of headhunting, the Iban still retained a strong link to their memories as warriors eager to take possession of the power of their victims by an act of decapitation. My guide, an Iban himself, informed me that the heads I would see in the longhouses, even though withered and unrecognizable, were all capable of speaking to his people in a way which was clearly untranslatable.

"Though their lips may be sealed," the young man called Komona said, "each head renders at least one note of the song that is death."

Already I sensed that I was about to enter a forbidden region as my guide and team of paddlers propelled our canoe upriver towards Genshwai longhouse, where Komona informed me a venerable *lemambang* still lived contentedly in the bosom of his family. He was the last of a line, the living relic of a tradition that formulated words from things without recourse to any form of discursive thought. According to Komona, he was still able to fashion a word from bamboo or from a flower or even a monkey's paw, and so make it sound entirely new. As he spoke of such things I could not help feeling as if a feather had been brushed lightly across my stomach.

Invariably, I began to think of certain expressions that previously I had seen as no more than a turn of phrase. The expression "to lose one's head," for example, took on a whole new meaning for me since our earlier conversation, in that it prefigured a sudden and irreparable loss of self as the result of a warlike act. I pondered this conundrum with more than a little interest. After all, if one's mouth and mind could be removed from one's body in the heat of battle, then it was reasonable to assume that words

78

could, in fact, be severed from being by way of an act of brutality too. It begged the question, of course: If words had the power to wound, could they not adequately protect themselves? Swords, daggers, and poisoned arrows flashed through my thoughts. I started to see them as words, all of them pointed, rather than as objects.

The Genshwai longhouse came into view after a day's paddling from the coast. When we finally went ashore our party was met by the village elders who welcomed us with a drink of *tuak,* a potent brew of rice wine that left me feeling somewhat intoxicated. I sat in the longhouse beside a basket full of severed heads hanging from the rafters. Each one was blessed with its own unique expression in death. For some strange reason I gained the impression that their absent torsos were waiting for them in serried ranks outside the longhouse. Komona informed me that it mattered little whether these men were present in "body and mind," or whether they had "lost their souls" in an act of thoughtless bravado. Either way, their severed heads bespoke an act of severance in that they were "gone but not forgotten."

Meanwhile I was introduced to an elderly man named Wrinkye whose ear-lobes, I noted, hung down almost to his shoulders. His skin was smooth and unwrinkled, while his ribs and clavicle protruded through paper-thin skin. I began to see him not as an elderly man so much as a piece of parchment. Nonetheless, he nodded courteously to me after Komona concluded his remarks on my reason for visiting his longhouse. As a *lemambang,* he was more than conscious of his role as an interpreter of things.

"You sir," he began, pausing to allow Komona to translate his remarks for me, "are welcome in our humble home in the forest. The trees, the vines, the creatures of the forest and all its variety of orchids are pleased that a scholar has at last come to study their language."

"I had no idea," I began, "that these objects actually communicated."

Wrinkye looked at me with a quizzical expression on his face, as much as to say, "Do you think that the forest is dumb?" Finally he produced a cloth bag and emptied its contents on the floor of the longhouse. Numerous strips of wood, reminiscent of wafers, tumbled forth, arranging themselves like fiddlesticks on the mat. I wondered then whether he was inviting me to join him in a game.

"These strips of wood we call story boards," he explained. "We allow them to arrange themselves into a sentence that reflects the mood of the day. Thus, when I toss them in a haphazard fashion like this"—Wrinkye flung the strips of wood at random on the mat. "You see, already we have a story from the forest."

I gazed at the story boards on the mat. I could perceive nothing in their arrangement except a random series of marks on the pieces of wood.

"The marks you see are a conversation from the forest," Wrinkye explained. "Today, they are telling us that the omen birds also wish to welcome you into their domain."

"The omen birds?"

"They are the first speakers of the forest. It is from their cries that words are constructed."

I was nonplussed. Our conversation was going nowhere. Pieces of wood that articulated the prognostication of birds—all this struck me as being derived from a fantasy world. I had no way of judging whether Wrinkye was attempting to trick me, or whether his world was in fact measured by other considerations. Then it struck me: I was dealing with an order of reality that was unpredicated. For the Iban people, the idea of a causal link existing between language and thought was inconceivable. For them, every word *grew* out of their experience with the forest. Now I knew what my friend had been trying to say when he told me that the Iban had gone beyond words in their engagement with nature.

I don't know whether it was the effects of the *tuak,* but increasingly I felt myself drifting into a netherworld of verbal sensations. Wrinkye's remarks had certainly stimulated my imagination to the point where I became conscious of wandering beneath a canopy of branches so greenly worded that to describe it would be to divest it of all linguistic nuances. The truth was that I was having trouble extricating myself from a pot-pourri of images: wild orchids, paddles flashing in sunlight, decapitated heads bundled in baskets, monkeys dancing along boughs, pigs nuzzling among refuse at the foot of ladders, Chinese vases graced with dragons and filled with rice, everything I had happened to gaze upon in the past few days now seemed to fuse in my mind, causing it to overflow with a mysterious kind of exuberance. I had become victim to a random array of story boards on which indecipherable markings were transformed into a series of hypnotic images. The green and entangled forest of liana that was the world of the Iban was now a part of me, its florescence undermining my own.

"May I ask a question of you, Mr. Wrinkye," I ventured.

"As our guest, this longhouse and its omen birds are here to serve your needs," Komona translated Wrinkye's reply.

"I wish to know whether your language was created by and for the benefit of your people, or whether it is a spontaneous creation of the rainforest."

"How can I answer that?" Wrinkye gathered up his story boards and placed them back in their bag as he spoke. "All I know, good sir, is that words are beetles that inhabit the undergrowth of our minds. They creep about under the leaves of our perceptions, regurgitating everything in their path. They consume what we do not see, yet nonetheless is itself important to the overall health of the forest. The Iban language is humus; it renders fertile what otherwise might remain an arid arrangement of things. Our forest is not made up of animals, insects or trees, no sir, not at all. It is made up of the timeless accumulation of objects that *masquerade* as concepts. Let it be known that we Iban consider our thoughts to be cluttered not with words but with the sweet poetry that each creature or object reveals when our senses embrace all its beauty and integrity."

I gazed at the severed heads in the basket hanging from the rafters. Now I knew why each expression on their faces was so different. They had died in the act of uttering their last word in life. I tried to imagine what it would be like to say "orchid," "paddle," "fish," "bird," or "forest deer" for the last time. I tried to imagine what it would be like to be savagely dismissed from the domain of objects that were words through a blow from a machete. I realized at once that this would be harder to bear than the cessation of breathing itself. Life-blood was not blood so much as language itself. It alone permeated and nourished being because it translated objects into sentiments, into experience.

"Sir," Wrinkye began, tying the cloth bag filled with story boards, using a piece of woven string to secure it. "I would like you to have these as a gift from the people of the Genshwai longhouse to honor your visit. A few random words are all we have to give a guest. They represent our lifelong encounter with the mystery of the forest."

I thanked Wrinkye, knowing at last what it was like to receive something more precious than words. I had heard for the first time the talk of the trees.

Journey to the East

In 142-, an Italian merchant named John of Pisa took ship to Jaffa in the Holy Land, en route for the eastern port of Goa. He planned to join a flotilla of vessels leaving the Gulf of Akaba for India. There he hoped to purchase a cargo of cloves and cinnamon before returning to Pisa. Quitting Jaffa, he traveled overland to Damascus in order to join a caravan traveling to the Gulf. Unfortunately, when he arrived in that fair city, he was told that the season for desert travel had already concluded. John was forced to make a decision. Either he must bide his time until the next year, or set out with his servant on a privately funded journey.

The prospect seemed daunting enough. Still, the lure of purchasing a cargo of spices and so make his fortune became his overriding consideration. Hiring a small number of camels along with their handlers, John set out on a journey across what he assumed would be vast reaches of sand towards Akaba. Little did he know, however, that after receiving misleading information as to the exact route because of the mendacity of his guide, he would find himself about to take the wrong direction near the remote trading town of Asaphara. Instead of traveling south-east to the Gulf, John soon found himself wandering through an unknown land that would forever change how he saw the world.

Herewith is his account of what he saw in that land:

Realizing that I had been deceived by my guide, and knowing not how to return to Damascus, I decided to press on, trusting in the name of the good Lord to protect and succor us. What else could we do but render ourselves into His care?

Soon we encountered naked men clothed only in the hair on their bodies. They were not aggressive but rather lewd in their every gesture. I was appalled when confronted by one of them in the act of copulation with a female member of his clan. He lay her over a rock, her buttocks pointing skyward, and penetrated her as if he were a plough and she the earth. I half expected her to cry out. Instead she whinnied like a mare in the company of a stallion. It seems that bestiality and licentiousness for these creatures was an act of bravado: their passions assumed the proportion of an extenuating and public demonstration of pleasure.

Passing beyond this land of barbarity and license, the first village that we encountered was populated by men who all seemed to be afflicted by a limp. It was strange to see them wandering towards their fields with one arm over their beasts of burden. At a distance they looked like centaurs with five legs, plodding forth to attend their crops. My servant, whose intelligence belied his worth sometimes, commented that these villagers had made their condition into a norm: each man vied with his neighbor in order to appear the greater cripple. All these men, I decided, were victims of a desire to seem less able than they were.

We soon journeyed through a narrow pass between rocky pinnacles. Here the sun barely reached the ground. Above us strange creatures of flight looped and glided among the crags. They were not birds so much as animals of indescribable countenance. Their droppings that rained down on us were sticky and black, like tar. A number of our cameleers were smitten by these missiles as we passed under them, and their skin rose in welts. No amount of swabbing with a solution of salt could alleviate their pain. The men informed me that it felt like they had been bitten by an adder. At night, as we lay about the fire, I could hear their cries of anguish. They were men mutilated by the excrescence of the devil.

On the other side of this pass we entered a wide plain blessed not with the warmth and clarity of the sun, but with a miasma of bluish light. I cannot describe it other than to say that even our skin took on the hue of cobalt. We were, in a sense, men besmirched with the color of darkness. We wandered about as if blind to one another. I suspect we were. None of us wished to acknowledge that in our hearts we were like men denuded of the warmth of human kindness. It was as if we had shed all contact with our past. Now we *were singular entities confronting the dark night of being, a Godless world stricken by harpies that were none other than ourselves.*

Presently we came to a walled city. At first I thought it a mirage. When we approached the gates they opened unaided, swinging slowly backwards on iron hinges. Above the entrance birds of prey were perched on the wall, their talons as sharp as scimitars. Who among us was not fearful as we entered the streets of this city? Yet the people were indifferent to our presence. It was as if they could not see us. We had become shades in the eyes of men, mere ghosts afflicted with the disease of wandering. They allowed us to pass along narrow alleys filled with stalls in which men sat, their eyes glowing like coals. There was a vacancy in their expressions, as if these people had passed over and were now living out a replica of past lives. I was reminded of Our Lord's descent into Hell: he alone could give back life to them and so refurbish their souls.

As we passed through these alleys I had the sensation of floating down a river on a raft. Everything slipped by so slowly that the life observed there seemed to be in a state of suspended animation. At one point we entered the Street of Scribes. Each booth was occupied by a man sitting cross-legged before his writing stool and pens. Behind him, rolls of parchment were piled one upon another. At one point a scribe withdrew a roll from his library and slowly unraveled it in order to read. I noticed at once that the text was written in an indecipherable language. Was it Sanskrit, Farsi, or indeed the letters of some Oriental alphabet that I had heard about from travelers but not seen myself? The truth was that for some strange reason I had lost the power to understand.

Then one of the scribes addressed me, reading from his scroll. That its indecipherable text was communicable astounded me. I heard his words echo around my mind like bees returning to the hive. His invocation was like a pullulating stream of epithets: each one damned my body, my presence, indeed my very existence in no uncertain terms. I had become like scum floating on the surface of a cesspool. The scroll had ascribed to me all the characteristics of a maggot. I was there to cleanse the wound that I had inflicted upon myself.

Soon we found ourselves passing through a cemetery littered with open graves and coffins lying about on the surface. It was as if in this place alone the Resurrection had occurred. Skeletons were strewn on the ground, each a bundle of whitened bones. It all looked so familiar. I had no hesitation in believing that what lay before me was the detritus of the human condition. When it came down to it, I told myself, I, John of Pisa, am no more than a coalescence of moments as if crystallized in my present body. Time is of my essence. As it passes, so do I enter into a stage of detumescence that prefigures my transition into all the fluidity of death. Ah! I told myself, I long for this moment. I have become a remnant of who I am.

Our tiny caravan passed through the city without incident. Before us lay a shimmering heat-haze. It reminded me of a drunken forest, these empty columns of warmth. As we surrendered to its capacity for obfuscation, I allowed my thoughts to wander. I had started out on this journey to a far country to purchase spices in order to make my fortune. I had ventured forth from the security of my home in Pisa, braved danger on the high seas, and placed myself in the dubious care of brigands and thieves, only to find myself wandering aimlessly in a land without identity or purpose. It was a place where my capacity to make judgments and to assess the predictability of my observations had been called into question. I too had become a mirage, lost in the deep deception of nature at its most playful.

Then I sensed that it was no longer I who was traveling through the desert, but another. I had become a disembodied being whose capacity for feeling was increasingly tenuous. I started to believe then that it was not I who had taken the wrong turning outside Asaphara. This "other" who had done so was, in fact, a man who regarded himself as a successful merchant and an upright member of his guild in Pisa. But the truth was that I was no longer that person. I had become instead someone whose soul was abyssal, adrift now in the indwelling vagaries of the universe.

Could it be, I told myself, that this land through which we were traveling was in some way a dream? Could it be that what we thought we had seen or experienced along the way was but a distillation of all the places and people previously known? It occurred to me that I had been too ready to regard far-flung Arabia and its provinces as an alien land populated by my own *prejudice and opinions, rather than by the emerging inwardness of my life. It was I who was seeing things differently, perceiving the world anew through the veil of appearance which I had previously accepted as its legitimate representation. Now at last it had been torn away. Now the true world was beginning to emerge from behind this deceptively real curtain of categories. Through a miracle, it seemed, I had survived the trap inadvertently set by the schoolmen of old.*

As our tiny caravan topped a rise, we recognized in the distance a low mountain filled with empty caves. Needing to water our camels, as it has been some days since we had camped in any oasis, we decided to make for this mountain in the hope of finding a well. At dusk we shielded our eyes, looking for that spring. It was then that I noticed a man descending from one of the caves with a water-bag over his shoulders. With luck, I thought, he would lead us to the Promised Land!

The man stopped when he saw us approach. We climbed down from our camels and made ourselves known to him through our interpreter. This man, whose countenance was both remote yet agreeably tranquil in its fixity and presence, offered to guide us to a spring to water our stock. In turn, I volunteered to carry his water-bag back to his house, which I presumed was located in a village on the mountain.

It was then that the man informed me he lived a hermit's life dedicated to God. I was taken aback. I had heard tell of these anchorites of the desert, men who sought the company only of themselves and their God, but never expected to meet one so deep inside the land of Arabia. He told me also that according to his knowledge of the terrain beyond this mountain, he alone lived "at the edge of the world." Nor did any man live beyond this point.

Hearing this, I was overcome by a feeling of melancholy. It was hard for me to accept that what lay beyond was a state of absolute emptiness, a dunghill of distorted and unruly forms. To turn back also seemed like a fool's choice. Nothing could persuade me from the belief that the country through which we had traveled so far would be as it had been, if ever we decided to return the way we had come. All of it had been the product of my mind's fancy, a terminal illusion and sleight-of-hand. I had allowed myself to be seduced by the idea of creating my own world when in reality its essential nature remained separate from all interpretation.

Because of my encounter with the anchorite, I suddenly realized that what I had passed through was a macabre form of enchantment. This, surely, was the result of a mental aberration on my part. If one were to remain in hell, it meant that one's punishment was to repeat ad nauseam *the incomplete gestures of one's life.*

I decided then that we had no choice but to press on, trusting in the good Lord to protect us. Emptiness, I concluded, was not so much a state of vacuity but the realization of what the schoolmen called a quintessence, whereby space, time, length, breadth and depth were finally translated into a lasting image of the Divine. It was true, I told myself, God does not see us or the world. He remains entrenched behind what is seen . . .

The manuscript ended at this point. There was no indication of how John of Pisa had extricated himself from his strange peregrination across the harsh sands of the Arabian Desert and beyond. We have no idea whether he reached Akaba or made the voyage to Goa. One must presume that he did so, otherwise why would he have written down what he had witnessed? Unless, of course, it was all part of a deliberate attempt to confuse his readers about what he had actually experienced. It may be that John's escape into that vast prism of emptiness, where everything and nothing is so delightfully refracted, had turned out to be more rewarding than all the spices of India put together, for it had alerted him to the true nature and mystery of things. Perhaps he had learnt how to sleep, and so turn his mind away from the very existence of the world.

Abelard's Epistle

Some time in the spring of 1115, the noted theologian, philosopher and poet, Peter Abelard, was attacked in his room and castrated by three men in the pay of Canon Fulbert, uncle to maid Heloise, with whom she resided in Paris. Abelard had been asked to teach Heloise theology and Latin, and accordingly took up residence in the canon's household to be near his pupil. The combination of her youth, beauty and intelligence, as well as long evenings by candlelight spent in her company disputing the possible existence of Universals, inevitably led to a growing intimacy between them.[1] Finally, unable to control his passion any longer, Abelard seduced the young woman, who was barely of age, even as he was seduced by her keen yet unformed intellect.

Deeply offended by such a blatant act of betrayal on the part of his lodger, Fulbert plotted his revenge. Nor could Abelard's secret marriage to Heloise, made in an obvious attempt to assuage the family's anger as well as to preserve his reputation as a teacher at the cathedral school in Paris, divert him from his course of action. On a warm spring night in 1115 it seems that Abelard lost not only his manhood, but the prospect of a long and brilliant career at the school as one of the greatest teachers of his age.

The subsequent scandal left Abelard in no doubt that his life had been changed forever. Deeply disillusioned by what had happened and, moreover, his own less than honorable behavior, he retired to a hut in the forest outside Paris to pursue a life of solitude. He urged Heloise to enter

---

1. A Universal was regarded as a quality, or property that each individual member of a class of things must possess if the same general word was to apply to all the things in that class. Redness, for example, is a universal possessed by all red objects. In contrast, the nominalists asserted that universals are nothing more than mere words. Abelard in his own logical writings brilliantly elaborated an independent philosophy of language. While showing how words could be used significantly, he stressed that language itself is not able to demonstrate the truth of things (*res*) that lie in the domain of physics.

a convent at Argenteuil on the Seine as soon as their child, Astrolabe, was born and placed in the care of his family. Reluctantly Heloise entered the convent, there to ponder the wreckage of her young life as the secret bride of one of the most brilliant intellects in France. Between them they had sought to discover a unity of purpose through a mutual engagement of minds, only to run aground on the shoals of their own bodies struggling to realize a unity of a more insistent nature.

In his forest retreat, under the eye of jackdaws perched in the tree above, Abelard attempted to draw comfort from the knowledge that the great second-century Alexandrian theologian, Origen, had also become a castrate like himself, yet still he had managed to live an exemplary life as a thinker and man. Even if Origen's mutilation was self-inflicted, he had wanted to make his status as a eunuch serve his dream of becoming a model Christian, whereby passion was forever eliminated as a motive for his actions.[2] In an effort to emulate his predecessor, and conscious of the anguish experienced by Heloise in her monastic retirement at Argenteuil, Abelard decided to write a letter to his great love in an attempt to explain to himself and to her the nature of their suffering. Taking a stool outside under the tree one morning, Abelard penned the following epistle:

My Beloved Sister in Christ,

It is hard, I know, to deal with our common fate. Lost in the unseemly fastness of our desire for one another, at a time when our bodies promulgated a language that we both thought might transcend even the language of Universals, we now find ourselves forced into the realization that a life of abstinence has become our destiny. We are bound, dear Heloise, star of my disordered passion, by the knowledge that divine conjugality and the marriage of the heart are no longer our lot. Whatever passion we knew when our bodies

---

2. It is said that Origen, as a young man, castrated himself so as to work freely in the task of instructing female catechumens.

*became joined, whatever caresses we responded to as cubs do
to a lioness's familiar and loving tongue, we are nonetheless
condemned for the rest of our lives to the exquisite pain of
never knowing anything other than the act of withholding.*

*As Dido died in the memory of Aeneas, so must you die in
me, dear Heloise. The walls of Troy no longer offer us succor.
The flames of pleasure to which we so readily abandoned
ourselves have become ashes, cold and unregenerate. They
no longer bear the heat of our love. We are as if immersed
in a cauldron of tears shed in memory of an experience now
forsaken forever—that of the perfect configuration of our
bodies entwined, like ivy on a chapel wall. From hereon, we
can but draw a curtain over this briefest and most poignant
of episodes, when tenderness and ecstasy mingled so readily
in our souls. This, surely, is what Dido felt as she watched
Aeneas sail away from Carthage in order to fulfill his destiny
as the founder of Rome.*

*I say these things in the knowledge that you suffer
as I do. More, perhaps—in that my potency is no longer,
whereas your yearning will go on just so long as your body
craves mine. I carry the bitterness of this fact deep in my
bosom. If there were power in heaven to make things other
than they are, then I would ask of it for your sake. But I
cannot. I am one condemned to a passion for language over
that of the exquisite prose of your body. Words have become
my puissance—while for you, my solicitude and cherished
moment, there can only be heartfelt recollection and a
conversion to the meaning of the Word itself. This is all I
can offer.*

*Such is the nature of our predicament. We were brought
together by Latin and the authors of antiquity, and divided
by a dagger. We became entranced under the gaze of Venus,
knowing that what we were engaged in was both a spiritual*

adventure and a journey into the primeval reaches of our capacity to think and to feel. We had made our minds and our bodies into scepters able to bestow nobility upon our every gesture. Prince and princess of Love, we bestrode the firmament like satyr and nymph together. Nothing stood in our way save the approbation of those who were eager to bring us down. Let me assume, then, that we are victims of the plague of their resentment. Its buboes fester on our bodies even as we struggle to survive the enormity of their crime against us!

I am and always will be yours, Heloise, sun and moon of my life. But from hereon I am condemned to the infinite solitude of being without a place to live, whereby my body and my mind wrestle as did Jacob with the angel. He, you see, was unsure whether to ascend the ladder in his pursuit of perfection, and so reach a state of Beyond, or whether to remain in mortal combat with the Divine Word. Until now, in my capacity as theologian and teacher, I have allowed myself to engage in such a battle. Hubris beckoned; it sought me out like a moth to the flame. In my reckoning I have been made a scapegoat to my passion. You, and only you, are its unwitting victim, since it is you who succumbed to my embrace through no fault of your own.

But enough of this! My rough forest hut is home to a new dispensation. My manhood, if such it be, is tempered by the realization that I have become a new man, one destined to remain in your life as more than memory only. Do not argue with fate for what it has dealt us. Do not disclaim such brief passion that has been ours in the name of some broken vow. You are my beloved wife through all eternity, even if we are separated by distance and circumstance. That I am your confessor goes without saying. There is nothing, no crime on earth that you need confess to me, however. You are perfection, the dark flower of obliteration, as well as the unending anguish that trust bestows upon all those who practice Love for its own sake. This, surely, is your great gift to the world.

I therefore tender you my fealty as a measure of my enduring respect for your person. If there be Universals, and I believe there are, then we are they. If there be Absolutes, then we partake of them. The heavenly vault above us is lit up by a luminescence that we alone bestow. It is we who erase darkness from the world because it is we who engender radiance through the love that we possess for one another. Our affections are not lightly bought, or indeed lightly given. Moreover I know, my fair Heloise, that for a brief moment time was made subservient to light as together we made dawn our crest.

Never forget that we were made one in Christ. He alone conferred His love of us in Him. Though I live alone in the forest caring for myself as best I can, I know that He is with me. The truth is, my beloved bride in Christ, that we are beholden to the dark obscurity of the Word, that templum to all existence. To enter into it is to embark upon a voyage into the meaning of what we mean to one another. For it is a fact that I confused the illusion of our passion, and therefore the integrity of your being, with my desire to meld body into mind—into our minds—once and for all. I began to believe that it might be possible to orchestrate a new human dispensation, whereby we, as divinely ordered opposites, would become primarily one in the One. As a result, and to my cost, your uncle saw fit to deprive me of my multiplicity, my being as a man. While I might harbour bitterness towards him, I am bitter toward me as well. It is I *who inflicted this fate upon myself, not he.*

You, my Heloise, are innocent of any crime. Our child Astrolabe is, unfortunately, also left alone because of my hubris. He will never know the common love of parents, or the prospect of our encouragement towards his maturity that goes with being so. He will grow up in the shadow of this stark event that deprived us both of our conjugality. Satiety, it seems, was our downfall. I ask only that you forgive me this fate that I have brought upon you. Aberrant behavior is often the partner of a keen intellect, it seems. I do not tender this as an excuse for my behavior, but as a fact.

There can be no greater loss to the world than the knowledge that chastity is a pure and honorable estate. By force of circumstance, we, dear Heloise, have become exemplars of this exalted condition. I count it a blessing from God that He has allowed us to have experienced at least a taste of His divine love for all beings in our mutual love. At least we are now conscious of the Great Fire that lies below the surface of the human condition, there to consume us at the appropriate moment. Inadvertently, we were made tinder to His passion.

Is it any wonder that we became removed from the lot of common men as a consequence? We are, dearest Heloise, but flotsam on the surface of the world. We float willy-nilly on the ocean that is time and space, forever embroiled in the turbulence of their inner dimension. No one knows what constitutes this condition save the Divine Word itself. But we must assume that it craves the consummation of our passion, even as it taunts us with its dissolution. The play of opposites, so dear to the philosophers of antiquity, is the game that we alone have played out to its limit.

So, fairest of all women, mistress of my soul, bear what is our absence from one another with fortitude and good grace. We are destined not to live together in this world, but to preside over emptiness pregnant with solicitude and love. This is the lot of all true lovers. They do not and cannot live in this world, but in another created by themselves alone. The Word decrees that we must perpetrate an inner passion[3] upon ourselves, one whose transformative power will make us incandescent with a strange and imageless love. In truth we will no longer see one another. We will have become consumed by the Word itself. Thus our unimagined being will be like stars glowing in the darkness of the heavens as a pure and distant light. Then, and then only will we have realized the true nature of our love.

I close this letter to you with my heartfelt wishes for your good health and wellbeing in the name of our Lord Jesus Christ. These words that I have penned today are like tears on the cheeks of Sophia, the goddess of Wisdom. They are moist with a detached love for Truth as it is expressed in the polarity of our being. Nothing stands between us now save the years of this earthly life that are left to us. Then we will once more be able to savor what was, momentarily, of another, unearthly order. I fondly believe, Fairest of All, that we will one day share the same cloister above and beyond this world.

Your husband in Christ,
Petrus Abelardus

There is no record of any reply to this letter from Heloise. But we do know that Abelard died in 1142, and was buried sometime later in the Convent of the Paraclete, which he founded near Argenteuil. Heloise became abbess of the Paraclete after she was expelled from Argenteuil in

3. The French expression *misticite amere* could equally be translated to mean "bitter or unrequited devotion."

1118. She was later buried in the nunnery grounds alongside Abelard in 1163. Even in death the lovers' peregrinations did not end, however. Their remains were moved no less than five more times over the centuries, until they were finally placed in their present resting place at Père-Lachaise cemetery in Paris.

The Skin of the Tiger
(in homage)

It was reported by Jorge Luis Borges, in one of his short stories, that a certain text written on the skin of a tiger (on all tigers, one suspects), which he called, parenthetically, the "script of the tiger," could, when uttered aloud, imbue the reader with a powerful sense of omnipotence, to the point where nothing might stand in his way.[4] According to Borges, the text was made up of fourteen random words, which in turn might be broken down into forty syllables. How they were uttered was not important; their random nature seemingly went beyond contexuality to embrace a dream of divinely ordered felicity that ensured any man who uttered them an inordinate sense of his own wisdom and knowledge. Unfortunately Borges—at least, the narrator in his story—did not reveal the formula contained by these words. It was left to the reader to surmise what the script of the tiger might invoke.

It begged a question, of course. How could any fourteen words, in whatever order they happened to be uttered, possibly trigger a man's transformation beyond that of the constraints of normal, everyday existence, unless of course they were of some magical import, as in the case of those pronounced by Ali Baba in the *Thousand and One Nights.* The suggestion that to utter "Open Sesame" might invoke an invisible force, or power able to open the door to a treasure trove could well be seen as an act of omnipotence, in that sesame-seed was commonly known to embody mystical properties. And, moreover, we know that special formulas and rigidly prescribed modes of diction such as "abracadabra" were often used by magicians to demonstrate their possession of unusual powers.

---

4. Jorge Luis Borges, "The Writing of the God," in *Collected Fictions*, (New York: 2004), 250-254.

I might have dismissed Borges' conundrum as the product of a flight of fancy, the whimsy of a great writer perhaps, had I not recalled a similar observation made by the ancient Greek philosopher and sage, Anaxagorus (c.500–428 B.C.), when commenting upon the origin of the universe.[5] He proposed the idea that all existents, including the stars, matter, nature, life, the process of birth through death, composition and reconstitution—these came about because of the random activity of invisible properties, which Aristotle termed *homoeomeries,* and that Anaxagoras likened to dust-like particles moving about space in a disordered fashion, all jostling one another, much as swallows appear to do when they flit about a barn. Out of this seeming random state of chaos a definite action was initiated which brought about the beginning of creation in the universe.

How did this process begin? Again Anaxagoras had an answer. He proposed the presence of a self-activating agent that he called the *nous.* The *nous* was a free and undirected energy, a mind that *self*-thought, thereby establishing a regime of random movements of Aristotle's so-called homoeomeries or "seeds of things" in the universe, which ultimately resulted in the act of creation as we know it.[6]

The *nous* did not direct this activity so much as it initiated the event by way of random movements in a cosmic game of chance. This cosmic game was driven by motion, whereby an indefinite number of paradigms was set up capable of embracing all of creation. Nietzsche likened this process to a game of dice: "the dice are always the same, but falling now this way, now that, they signify different things for us."[7] It appears, at least from Anaxagoras's and Nietzsche's point of view, that the *nous* was a form of cosmic crap game enabling the realization of multiple revelations, while remaining itself ever the same.

So now we have at least two notions of random activity to account for an all-powerful act of creation. One is made up of the sum of fourteen words; the other of the activities of an infinite number of so-called "seeds of

5. Parts of a whole that is like its parts.
6. Compare Anaxagoras's fragment: "Mind is infinite and self-powerful and mixed with nothing, but it exists alone itself by itself."
7. See *Philosophy in the Tragic Age of the Greeks,* (Washington: 1962).

things" moving this way and that. One is made up of forty syllables written on the skin of a tiger and pronounced by a man; the other of mysterious dust particles stirred into life by an equally mysterious entity known as the *nous.*

For a person like myself, given to thinking in a logical fashion, both these notions seemed to be fraught with implications not easy to accept. The skin of a tiger resembling an occult formula: it sounded absurd. A detached mind randomly directing dust particles in the hope of determining form in matter—was this no more than a primitive scientific theory? If I considered the former proposition, what came to mind was a tiger's skin moving in consonance with its muscles, thereby changing at any given moment. If I thought of the latter, then I had a vision of order fatally flawed by inconceivable and arbitrary movement, like that which one sees looking down into the streets from high above a city.

Either way, I remained skeptical as to the entire process of reasoning displayed by both men. It seemed to me that Borges and Anaxagoras had failed to sustain their argument.

Which made me wonder why seemingly intelligent men as Borges, Anaxagoras and Nietzsche had arrived at so similar a conclusion! Were they, in some way—and across time—in collusion? Were they attempting to fashion an omnipotent reality, which was always the same, out of entirely different propositions? A tiger's skin with its tawny markings, a self-activating mind that, when it trembled, caused the universe to be, and an unpredictable dice that, when thrown, turned up different numbers while remaining itself—these were such unusual analogies that I began to wonder whether words in some way—or at least images—had interposed themselves between how creation occurred and our perception of that event. Fourteen randomly uttered words seemed a far cry from such theories as the Big Bang, the Black Hole, or some other astronomic cataclysm as a method of unleashing celestial order upon the universe, hypothetical or otherwise. Or was Borges suggesting that words, in themselves, were explosive?

I began to suspect this is indeed what he meant. In his usual allusive way, Borges had wanted his readers to recognize that the skin of a tiger was in some sense a veil behind which other realities were at work. The combination of forty syllables could be arranged into an infinite number of words, all of which might evoke some magical formula, or formulas, whose intent was to change the nature of the world. This was no verbal crap game as I had assumed, but a version of what might best be called "tautological thinking," when the miracle of one thing was replicated by another.

The tiger's skin with its tawny markings was thus a palimpsest upon which an immeasurable number of expressions could be written, each a possible revelation of the inexpressible mystery of creation. Clearly Borges was attempting to re-write creation in his own image. He, like Ali Baba, had found a way of opening the door to a treasure trove.

Now I felt that I was onto something. The mystery surrounding the tiger's skin, and those unlikely dust particles, was beginning to coalesce in my mind to form a pertinent statement about a man's inability to claim for himself the power of transformation otherwise available to him, unless he were prepared to embrace the idea of disorder, disunity, and chaos as positive attributes. I had come to the realization that both Borges and Anaxagoras were barking up the same tree. They wanted me to understand that words and images, though entirely inadequate, were nonetheless important to the business of encountering knowledge as a mystical property.

Indeed, a tiger's skin and dust particles were like Ali Baba's invocation: they had the power to pave the way through the labyrinthine passageways of the mind towards that indestructible core at the centre of one's being. Borges and Anaxagoras, I decided, were men on a mission—to transform reality by way of thought manifesting itself as images.

So that's it! The surface of reality was no more than an infinite arrangement of images. This, of course, invariably appeals to the eye, seduced as it is by endless and unlimited formations. But what lay below its surface could be invoked only by a randomly conceived formula, an invocation perhaps, that was both arbitrary and yet entirely senseless. This—shall I call it subterranean knowledge?—was stimulated towards existence by way of the nous, of mind or thought, which in turn was stimulated by the magical surface of reality.

Thus, there was a correspondence between the deceptive nature of surface reality and the inner core that precipitated it. Anaxagoras argued that this is because the nous participates in materiality, in illusion, and in multiplicity by way of separation. Mind sets things in motion, separates from them, and so allows them to become more distinct. It is as if an eagle has laid an egg, hatched it, and then pushed the fledgling out of the nest! The beauty of the visible world is therefore conditioned by the distance it has traveled from its origin.

A remarkable concept. Borges must have known it to be true, otherwise why would he have emphasized the random nature of a script buried in the skin of a tiger? He must have sensed that the tiger itself was in league with the arbitrary nature of language. As it moved, so do words become infinitely jumbled. To utter these logically would be to dismiss the pure inventiveness of the animal's stripes as they responded to its muscular movements while pacing its cage. It would seem, then, conversely, *that words are in league with the muscles of the mind.* As these engage with the world, so does language participate in the beauty and illusion of creation. There is therefore never any necessity to be concerned about the logic of expression when attempting to overcome the inherent difficulties of life. Ali Baba is proof of that. His statement, combining as it does a mystical seed and a verb attributed to a door swinging on its hinges ("Open, Sesame"), enabled him to access a treasure trove! Is there anything more illogical than that?

Now I begin to understand why it is that we resort to magical formulas when we engage with life. They are the stuff of the universe, the seething energy of dust particles invigorating the world. They latch onto things— eagles in their nests, an arctic flower blossoming at the edge of a glacier, even a spider at the bottom of its sand trap patiently awaiting its victim to fall in—and make them their own. In the end, I realized (as Borges must have done too), words are sticky, like sap. Moreover, they exude a life of their own, one distinct from the trunk that created them. The script of the tiger is none other than an elaborate artifice designed to enlist the illusory nature of things in order to satisfy our need for absolutes. It is why any invocation of this nature shall remain, throughout time, a mysterious concoction of words without rhyme or reason. In turn these should remind us, if we didn't know it already, that life is pretty much a jumble of a poem.

Butterfly Man

*I*n the spring of 195–, the noted Russian émigré and author, Vladimir Nabokov, set out for Nebraska and Wyoming in the foothills of the Rocky Mountains to collect butterflies. They had been a ruling passion of his ever since he was a boy on the family estate at Vyra, near St. Petersburg.

"From the age of seven, everything I felt in connection with a rectangle of framed sunlight was dominated by a single passion," he said, speaking of his obsession. "It is not improbable that had there been no revolution in Russia, I would have devoted myself entirely to lepidopterology."

It seems that this tiny creature, this "rectangle of framed sunlight" as he called it, represented for Nabokov a lifelong search for beauty unlike any other. His love of butterflies and later literature, moreover, framed the future conduct of his life. Probably he knew from an early age that the word for "butterfly" was derived from the same root-word as "soul" in his native Russian.

I was struck by this coincidence—that a man could spend his entire lifetime studying butterflies, while at the same time devoting himself to the careful arrangement of words into what we now acknowledge to be highly original works of literature.[8] Viewing an exhibit of butterflies in a museum cabinet is to see a singular correspondence, however. Are they not arranged in rows, much as words are on paper? Is it not possible to read the delicate arrangement of wings under glass, each as if a word, a phrase, that in turn speaks of color, diversity, and the innumerable facets of beauty of which nature alone is capable?

Nabokov probably recognized their similarity. In seeking out a new species of butterfly high in the Rocky Mountains as he did that year, he was in effect attempting to identify and capture the soul in words. The "glass

---

8. Books such as *Lolita* and *Pale Fire*.

cabinets" that housed his verbal collection were none other than his books.

Or could it have been some other motive that had inspired his lifelong search for butterflies and phrases? I was reminded of a dream related by Chuang Tzu,[9] the ancient Chinese sage, in which he identified himself with a butterfly:

> *Once upon a time, I, Chuang Tzu, dreamt I was a butterfly, fluttering hither and thither, to all intents and purposes a butterfly. I was conscious only of my happiness as a butterfly, unaware that I was Chou. Soon I awakened, and there I was, veritably myself again. Now I do not know whether I was then a man dreaming I was a butterfly, or whether I am now a butterfly, dreaming I am a man. Between a man and a butterfly there is necessarily a distinction. The transition is called the transformation of material things.*

It struck me, when reading of this remarkable dream, that Nabakov and Chuang Tzu felt something in common, in spite of the passage of time that lay between them: they were both men who by accident or design confused themselves with a creature that became themselves in the act of dreaming. More importantly, they were men who had recognized what Chuang Tzu considered a movement away from the idea of unique or singular identity into what he called a state measured by the "transformation of material things." In a sense, men could become what they were not, simply by dispensing with who they were. This dream within a dream was to do with breaking free from the chrysalis of being in order to possess wings of an entirely different order.

And what were these wings made of? Nabokov's obsession with butterflies was derived as much from the infinite variety that they presented to his eye, both in color and in shape, as to the quality, the intimation of translucency which they embodied. In spite of the richness and profusion

9. Chuang Tzu (Confucius) was China's most famous teacher, philosopher, and political theorist, whose ideas influenced the civilization of East Asia. Born in 551 B.C., Chuang Tzu saw reality as not revealed truth but as an expression of self-cultivation, of the ability of human effort to shape its own destiny. He is regarded as the first teacher in the ancient land of China.

of colors that they transmitted, their wings also suggested something harder to define. It was at this point that Nabakov became a writer. He recognized, even as a youth, that what he was drawn to in the butterfly was the tender opalescence, the gentle articulation of pattern, the incomparable wonder of color as an aerial phenomenon. To see so many colors and patterns dancing about as if manipulated by a puppeteer, was to imagine a cosmic dance. How was he to explain this to himself? How was he to note in his field journal a scientific—let's say, a lepidopterological—explanation for what lay passively at the bottom of his net? It was an impossible task.

As I remarked, it was at this point that Nabokov became a writer. He began to see in the butterfly an alliterative and possibly an onomatopoeic device. "My pleasures are the most intense known to man: writing and butterfly hunting," he wrote. This strange connection between words and wings, between an abstraction and an object, may well be considered as a pathological aberration, were it not that Nabokov was able to isolate their properties through multiple acts of literary creation as well as scientific analysis.

This does not mean, however, that he was able to isolate one from the other—that is, the butterfly from the metaphor—in his more private moments. I secretly believed that he longed to see these particular miracles of expression merge into one, visible, complex, and transformative thing or event, a kind of hyper-creature. If it were to occur, through his intervention as a writer or as a scientist, then there was a real possibility that he would have emulated Chuang Tzu's dream encounter, and so realized in himself a "transformation of things," whereby dream and reality became one.

One should not dismiss such a condition lightly as the product of a mind devoid of impartiality. Nabokov was a sophisticated and refined individual. He had studied art and science with equal fervor. When he drew his own butterflies, which were a product of his imagination only, he always managed to imbue them with an even more rarefied perfection than those in nature. Nabokov's butterflies transcended the real and overreached the ideal, becoming instead emblematic of his own mental state.

In drawing these tiny rectangles of light on letters to friends and as pictures on the covers of his books, he was attempting to transform reality in the way that Chuang Tzu meant it to be transformed. In the process a "Nabokov Blue," for example, became a form of linguistic image, whereby he was able to explain the interior perfection that he had somehow glimpsed within himself. In other words, the butterfly, which he pursued avidly in everyday life, became a device to unlock a translucency that lay like some chrysalis in the earth, ready to emerge into the world from the humus of his thoughts.

Nabokov sought in nature a language that was above nature—indeed, above the powerful and oracular function of language itself.

Chuang Tzu would have approved. The transformation of material things was at the heart of his philosophy. To be a butterfly or not to be a butterfly, this was the question. To flutter hither and thither as if in a dream was to give credence to the idea that a man was capable of utterly transcending his material condition. The soul in life was being released from its pupa, its earthy and inchoate environment. It was beginning to spread its wings. It was beginning to do what Chuang Tzu imagined himself to be doing in his dream—fluttering hither and thither with abandon. One suspects that this is merely an allusion to a more elevated condition. The mind had become a meadow at the foot of the mountains—the Rocky Mountains, no less!—where a certain fullness and freedom acted out its momentary life.

One can forgive Nabokov for having spent a good part of his spare time wandering in remote places looking for rare butterflies, just as one can forgive Chuang Tzu for having dreamt himself as one of these delightful creatures. Both men were enamored of the prospect of turning an object into some form of inward expression. Both men wanted to lose themselves in the dream of becoming this creature of incomparable beauty. In truth, had not these men attempted to make the transition from identity to a state of self-transcendence for the sole reason of defying the time, place, and predicament into which they were born?

To be a butterfly in a dream, or write a book blessed by its image, was to explore a dimension not open to everyone. For both men the butterfly implied so many transitions (so many enlivened souls) in the conduct of one's life, that not to be absorbed by them would be to diminish the whole process of existence.

I began to see Nabokov's love of words as a way through the miasma of divisiveness and displacement that characterized the events of his life. An exile, an émigré, a vagabond scientist and novelist, his many roles finally came together and were resolved in his love of butterflies. The freedom and beauty of their lives was in stark contrast to the constraint and difficulty of his own peripatetic existence, wandering from Russia to Cambridge, to Paris, Berlin and finally to America in search of a home.

The butterfly, he realized, did not have a home, either. Its habitat was marked by the realization of a certain beauty, which was in turn subject to the imperial edicts of duration. The creature lived for a brief time in air, in space, and in the domain of affectation. It shone, as if it was a rectangular prism of sunlight. Such a quality he longed to capture in words. And so, with words, he attempted to fill the vast cabinets of his mind with ideas capable of emerging from their chrysalis-like state into butterflies.

It was this condition that Chuang Tzu understood perfectly. He too had become a butterfly. Or in a dream he had been transformed into a butterfly dreaming of himself as a man. It made little difference. This remarkable Chinese sage had found a method that enabled him to transcend his predicament by entering so completely into the mind of a butterfly that any distinction, any material distinction at least, became irrelevant. The world of things had simply fallen away. The domain of duration was negated. And, moreover, the anguish of wandering from one state to another in search of an official post in China, a situation he had encountered throughout his life, was no longer capable of eroding memory.[10] This, he knew, was none other than the life of a butterfly. Hither and thither it flitted, a soul creature

---

10. Confucius served first as a magistrate, then as an assistant minister of public works, and eventually as minister of justice in the state of Lu. It is likely that he accompanied King Lu as his chief minister on one of the diplomatic missions. His loyalty to the king alienated him however from the power holders of the time, the large Chi families, and his moral rectitude did not sit well with the king's inner circle, who enraptured the king with sensuous delight. At 56, when he realized that his superiors were uninterested in his policies, Confucius left the country in an attempt to find another feudal state to which he could render his service.

always on the lookout for like souls. For a few short seconds (or was it a lifetime?) Chuang Tzu had metamorphosed into the creature of his dreams.

I began to realize that I had stumbled into one of the least illuminated chambers of the mind. Here men sought to reconcile the disparity between what they saw and what they imagined. I asked myself why it was that these worlds always seem to remain apart, as if they were trains passing at night. The lights in the carriages of each were but rapid transitions flitting past. Was this the way lives are, engaging with one another? Or is this vision of transitory light merely an intimation of what Nabokov and Chuang Tzu saw in a butterfly?

I cannot be sure. But what I begin to comprehend is that the soul has its own way of manifesting its presence. Whether as a butterfly or as a dream of a butterfly, there will always be some invisible correspondence. Clearly, the chrysalis of being is a worthy artifice in that it embodies both image and word. This is what Vladimir Nabokov set out to bring together in his work and his writings. He had tried to salvage from the debris of material existence a few pieces of ostraca that might give him guidance on how best to conduct himself as a butterfly, and as a man. This, I feel certain, is the true meaning of what he called a "rectangle of light."

All at Sea

Josephina's Café is located in a tiny square near Buenos Aires at the point where Avenida Juncal splits and becomes two roads. From my table on the pavement outside I can look up Juncal, past a marble statue of Venus rising nude from a garden, imagining myself standing in the bow of a ship as waves of traffic part before her gaze. Venus is the perfect figurehead. She seems to anticipate salt-spray and ocean troughs, white-caps and dolphins, even as she raises one arm in an anticipatory gesture towards trucks and buses.

I am beholden to her grace just as I am to the noisy tranquility of Josephina's. I could be at Trafalgar or at the mouth of the Nile, preparing to order a broadside at Napoleon's ships-of-the-line. The shot that I arm my cannon with, however, is the scything nature of words. I keep telling myself that they are capable of taking the wind out of most sails.

The thought that had been pre-occupying me over coffee that morning was an image of Orpheus's head drifting down the River Hebrus. It had been torn from his body by Thracian maidens after he unwisely refused their advances. It seems that he was still mourning the loss of his beloved Eurydice whom he had endeavored to rescue from Hades after she had inadvertently died from a snake-bite while attempting to escape the advances of another man. That he was able to persuade the gods in Hades to release her into his care is testament to his lyrical talent.

Orpheus, after all, had made song his principal weapon against all the powers of darkness. Still, it had not prevented him from ignoring the gods' injunction that he must not look back at Eurydice as he lead her back into the world. The gods of the dead once more claimed her, and Orpheus was left to mourn his loss, as well as contemplate the stupidity of his actions.

Before me lay Orpheus's head drifting down Juncal amid a stream of traffic. I was unable to get his decapitation by crazed maidens out of my mind. Mournful music coupled with the blare of car-horns, and rejected nymphs destroying what they most desired, filled my thoughts. Love and death joined in one mutilated image of hair—tresses, I think they are called—floating among words.

I was reminded also of the German word *liebestod,* which reflects a state of mind brought about when lovers die in a moment of ecstasy. Certainly Tristan and Isolde knew this moment well. Yet, for all that, I couldn't understand why Orpheus had been so thoughtless as to glance back at Eurydice, knowing that he had been forbidden to do so. Was it pride? Was it a mental aberration? Was it indeed . . . fear that motivated him? The song-maker, it seems, must have lost all sense of his limitations.

At this point an elderly gentleman, dressed in a grey suit and tie, approached the café and took a table nearby. He was smoking a very small but elegant pipe, which seemed to drift away from his mouth as if it wished to remain detached on a more permanent basis. I was so taken by this object that I remarked to him of the pleasure that it gave me. He responded in Spanish, then French, and finally in broken English. *Señor,* do you speak another language, he remarked? Hebrew, perhaps, or Armenian? In passing, and in a sort of jumble of words, he mentioned the massacre of Jews at Masada by the Romans, the historian Josephus celebrating their courageous stand, and the Alexandrian philosopher, Philo, trying to reconcile Platonism with the Bible.[11] This heady movement from one language to another, from one set of ideas to another, left me wondering whether we were not, in fact, speaking in tongues. I was in no doubt that the conversation we were about to have would be as vivid in memory as Orpheus's head floating down Juncal in a stream of traffic.

"You realize, of course," he said, "that it makes no difference whether we say anything that is at all remotely sensible."

---

11. Following the fall of Jerusalem and the destruction of the Second Temple (70 A.D.), the Masada garrison—the last remnant of Jewish rule in Palestine—refused to surrender and was besieged by a Roman legion. It took the Roman army of almost 15,000, fighting a defending force of less than 1,000, including women and children, almost two years to subdue the fortress. The Zealots, however, preferred death to enslavement, and the conquerors found that the defenders had taken their own lives.

I was taken aback by this remark, until I recalled Orpheus mingling words with water in the River Hebrus as he attempted to sing his plaints. To forestall further argument that we might have anything pertinent to say to one another, I told the gentleman of what I had been thinking about. In doing so, I asked him to consider what might have provoked Orpheus to make such a fatal mistake as to condemn his true-love to a second encounter with the gods of Tartarus.

"A contrast in personalities," the man responded in a mixture of languages. "In spite of their love for one another, which they obviously possessed to a very high degree, Orpheus and Eurydice allowed this love to conceal their inherent differences."

But theirs is a myth, I remonstrated, not a psychological encounter.

"You fail to understand what each of them represented to themselves. Orpheus is more than his name. It is an ancient word whose origin goes back into the mists of time. *Aur,* you see, means "light" or "radiance" in Greek, and *rophoe* that of "cheering good health." Thus, this poet that you speak of, this man of the lyre and the persuasive power of a god, irradiates our lives and promotes well-being with his every song. *Aurophoe* is not just a songster but one who configures language as an act of magic in our lives."

And his beloved Eurydice, I inquired, eager to complete the puzzle?

"Her name is made up of two qualities," the man added, pressing stray tobacco into the bowl of his pipe with a practiced gesture of his forefinger. He was warming to his position as Josephina's resident etymologist. "*Rohe* speaks of her vision, clarity and capacity to reveal what she knows. *Dich* informs us that she is a teacher, one who is able to convey what in the normal course of events remains a secret. Clearly *Rohedich* was a Sybil; her role is to advise and to show. She is a more contemplative person than Orpheus."

Does this mean, I asked, that he was an extravert who saw himself as above censure or subject to petty rules, even if they were those decreed by the gods in Hades?

"Now it is you who is resorting to psychological explanation!" the gentleman responded, his pipe glowing with renewed vigor. "You see how we are so ready to mix up our various thoughts? One moment these lovers are a part of mythology; the next they bear the burden of our personal inadequacies. *Aurophoe* and *Rohedich* are no longer Orpheus and Eurydice. Instead, these lovers embody a conflict between the exuberance of one versus a desire to help on the part of the other. Such a clash of personalities brought about the tragedy of a headless torso drifting downstream and a young woman condemned to a premature death because of her lover's importunity. Can you see now why it is impossible to believe in the truth of one language or word over another?"

Dear me, I thought. The gentleman with the pipe had managed to breach the swell on Juncal, causing Venus to glisten with the salty taste of words in the process. Her nudity was no match for this man's predilection to distort realities in the interest of drawing forth another perspective from the waves. Isn't this what Eurydice stood for, anyway? Was she not a woman of supreme diction, able to formulate purely and without contradiction a lasting image of her failure to escape death even if it were, in some ways, ecstatic? The Germans knew a thing or two about such strange modes of mutual annihilation in love, I told myself. So their knowledge of it was clearly pertinent to our present discussion.

"I am of the opinion, *señor*, Orpheus and Eurydice are but signs of our fascination with meaning. They linger in us as names, of course, but their real significance lies in their ability to transform our everyday reality into one extraordinary act of transcendence. Are we not on a voyage towards some infinite understanding? Are we not equipped with skills that make it possible for us to see and understand things in greater depth? The ocean, surely, is but a metaphor for how deep we are prepared to plunge. It makes little difference whether we speak in English, Spanish or French—or in Hebrew, if you so wish. Words, in any language, are like plankton floating about in the sea. As creatures they are numberless, and so speak to us of how nourishment for the whale is an act of infinitude. Words nourish us in the same way. They are like tiny insects, microscopic cells, atomic particles— all that is invisible to the eye, and yet so important to the conduct of life. It should not surprise you that the beauty we expect from words finds its palpable image in two lovers such as Orpheus and Eurydice."

"So that what we see is not always what we get," I mused aloud, trying to make some sense of a Greek myth which was an anagram merging with the rushing waters that was the traffic on Juncal. I thanked my lucky star that Venus was there to direct this torrent past our respective tables. As shipmates, too, we were about to do battle with the most subtle yet irresolute of enemies—that of our mind's failure to give due credence to the idea that artifice is one of the primary tools of understanding.

Meanwhile, I could barely contain my surprise at what the gentleman with his pipe had told me. The tale of Orpheus and Eurydice had been elevated to that of two contending arguments about trust, obedience, and the consequences of not respecting these. Not only were truth and knowledge condemned to a stygian existence in Hades, but the Great Song that was Orpheus had been torn to pieces for his lack of passion in the face of those ongoing forces of life as embodied by nymphs. I was confused. I was uncertain. Sitting in Josephina's, with Venus breasting the waves on Juncal, I felt myself drifting into a state of dyslexia: every word found itself reversed, turned upside down, re-invented, and finally distorted beyond recognition.

The history of the Jews, their battle with Rome, and a man's attempt to convert the Bible into a set of Platonic ideals, all these seemed to tumble about my ears. I was awash in a river of inversions, a noble head mournfully singing of its loss. Could I ever begin to understand why a man who was dismissive of language could bring forth from his mind something archaic—four words that combined to make two, which in turn invoked a myth about two lovers condemned to remain apart in this life? It didn't make sense—but then, this is precisely what the gentleman with his pipe had said might happen anyway!

"Let us then assume, *señor*," the gentleman interrupted my thoughts, "that you and I are victims of a profound and irrevocable confusion. I might have addressed you in any number of languages about the subject, and the answer would have always been different. Artifice is a pure ingredient, far purer than the exactitude of words. It clothes things, it creates illusion, it prepares us for our longed-for escape from the obvious. How could one not prefer two lovers and their star-tossed destiny to that of the prolixity of meaning as embodied by their essence? Unless words are transformed into images they are no more than limp objects, fishes on a pier, there to putrefy in the sun unless we prepare them in readiness for a banquet. I myself prefer *a la carte* to that of *plat du jour*. Variety, and an endless cornucopia of tastes, these are what make life worthwhile, surely."

I couldn't agree more. The trouble was, I still found myself identifying with Orpheus's severed head floating half-submerged in a river. It was a haunting image that not even coffee at Josephina's café could erase. For company I might have had Venus and this gentleman with his pipe, but still I was drawn to the memory of a songster who destroyed his great love through an act of disobedience and hubris. Was this the fate of all of us, I asked myself? Do we all look back at our greatest gift, fearful that it might no longer be there? I kept imagining myself in the pit of hell trying to get out. Would I have the courage to look ahead at all times, and simply trust? These questions drifted through my thoughts like Orpheus's hair in the waters of the Hebrus: everything seemed all in a tangle.

"In the final analysis, *señor*," the gentleman spoke above the roar of traffic. "We are in thrall to ancient instincts more powerful even than words. They accost us in the most unlikely moments. Like those men and women who jumped to their deaths at Masada, not wishing to give up their freedom, we too sometimes see ourselves leaping into the unknown. Neither historian nor philosopher has strength enough to stop us.

"All I have now is my pipe which acts as a comma, a pause to arrest the onrushing speed of my thoughts. The act of meditation becomes more fulsome and immediate, as you can imagine. I become detached, like Orpheus's head. Then I begin the task of rebuilding myself in my own image. It is at this point, *señor*, I come to accept that in life we are all—shall I say it?—linguistically alone. Words may be a balm, but in themselves they are not—let's call it . . . love. Do I make myself clear?"

Perfectly, I remarked. But I knew he was only partly correct.

Without the fraternity of words, would we ever begin to share the most elusive emotion of all, that of heartfeltness?

www.ingramcontent.com/pod-product-compliance
Lightning Source LLC
Chambersburg PA
CBHW060839250626
47162CB00005B/2110